Zoey had almost forgotten Lucas's news. She looked at her watch. 5:30. Lucas's new house guest had probably arrived. She turned onto South Street. Her curiosity piqued, Zoey decided to drop her stuff off at home and then go to Lucas's to get her first glimpse of Kate Levin.

As it turned out, she didn't have to wait that long. As she headed to her own front door, Zoey glanced up at the Cabrals' house. She squinted to make sure that the fading sun hadn't made her see things. But there were no two ways about it.

In the upstairs window, Zoey could see Lucas hugging a redhead. And even from this distance, Zoey could tell she was a very pretty redhead.

Don't miss any of the books in
Making Out
by Katherine Applegate
from Avon Flare

MAKING OUT #13

Don't tell Zoey

KATHERINE APPLEGATE

AN AVON  FLARE BOOK

AVON BOOKS, INC.
1350 Avenue of the Americas
New York, New York 10019

Copyright © 1996 by Daniel Weiss Associates, Inc., and Katherine Applegate
Published by arrangement with Daniel Weiss Associates, Inc.
Library of Congress Catalog Card Number: 98-93668
ISBN: 0-380-80869-2
www.avonbooks.com/chathamisland

First Avon Flare Printing: June 1999

AVON FLARE TRADEMARK REG. U.S. PAT. OFF. AND IN OTHER COUNTRIES, MARCA REGISTRADA, HECHO EN U.S.A.

Printed in the U.S.A.

WCD 10 9 8 7 6 5 4 3 2

Don't tell Zoey

Zoey

What is love? If you had asked me a year ago, or even six months ago, I would have probably said that love was a feeling, an overwhelming emotion that made you want to lose yourself in another person. Pretty corny, huh? At the time I was trying to write a romance novel, so maybe that explains something about my state of mind. I was also still going out with Jake, who, while being a great guy, wasn't exactly making my knees weak.

Now I'd say that that kind of passion is important, but it's not the only thing that love's about. Love is not just caring for a person; it's also understanding them.

1

If you really love and really understand someone, you can forgive things that, on paper, may seem pretty unforgivable.

Take, for example, my parents. They found out this fall that my father had another daughter. It wasn't as bad as it could have been. I mean, Lara came about before my parents were married, but it was still upsetting enough to drive my mother into the arms of another man. Now, if love were only about a passionate feeling, then they wouldn't have been able to work all of that stuff out. But they have. And they're almost more in love than ever—which can get pretty gross at times.

I guess you could say the same thing about me and

Lucas. It did start off as an uncontrollable, totally passionate urge that I couldn't fight, but it's definitely about more than that now. Especially since Lucas has forgiven me for giving in to a similar passionate urge with Aaron Mendel—something that could probably be considered the biggest mistake of my life. I can say for certain that I will <u>never</u> do anything like that again.

So, yes, love is still an overwhelming emotion and a physical attraction, but it's also about being with someone and accepting that they're not perfect. Which sometimes means accepting that they have physical attractions to other people. Unfortunately.

One

"Mmm, that feels good," Zoey Passmore said, closing her eyes and lying back on her bed. "Do it just a little harder."

Zoey sighed as her boyfriend, Lucas Cabral, continued to rub her feet. Helping out at her parents' restaurant was always exhausting, but that night it had been even worse than usual.

"I thought business was slow during the winter," Lucas said. "Why'd you have to stay so late?"

"Private party," Zoey replied.

"Fun," Lucas said.

"Yeah. It would've been even more fun if the dishwasher had been working."

On a normal Wednesday, Zoey tried to get home in time to watch *Party of Five*, but that hadn't even been a remote possibility this evening. The broken dishwasher had added an extra two hours of standing on her feet to Zoey's already long night of work. She still had homework left to do, but somehow, with Lucas massaging her arches, it was the last thing on her mind.

Zoey moaned. "Now I'm too tired to do homework."

4

"I know one way to wake you up," Lucas offered, a sparkle in his hazel eyes.

"Without caffeine?" Zoey laughed.

Knowing what Lucas had in mind wasn't very difficult, considering the fact that her boyfriend had a one-track mind. Even if they weren't in her room, lying on the bed with the door shut, Lucas would want to fool around. And though she wouldn't admit it, fantasizing about this very moment had gotten Zoey through scrubbing the dessert plates.

Lucas gently placed her foot down on the covers, put his hands on either side of her, and crawled catlike up the bed to where she lay. Without hesitation, he planted a kiss on her lips that sent shivers down Zoey's spine.

Just what I needed, Zoey thought, relaxing into the warmth of Lucas's touch. Kissing Lucas made everything—the rowdy customers, the broken dishwasher, the reading she had to do—slip from Zoey's consciousness. Lying on her bed with Lucas's arms around her, Zoey felt as if the whole world had disappeared.

How could she have almost given this up for another guy—any guy, much less that snake Aaron Mendel? Sure, Aaron was gorgeous and talented and said all the right things, but he could never hold a candle to Lucas in the kissing department. He could never make Zoey feel the blood drain from her head to her toes with a simple touch. Lucas was the only guy who had ever made Zoey feel this way. He was the only guy who ever would. Thank God he had forgiven her.

Zoey felt her kisses become more urgent, more intense. Lucas had been right. She was revitalized.

Suddenly Lucas pulled away. He lay next to her on the bed, their faces not even an inch apart. Zoey gazed into his eyes almost as intensely as he gazed into hers.

"I should go now," Lucas said, brushing a stray blond hair off her cheek.

Zoey stared back at him in amazement. Things were just heating up between them, as their messed-up clothes and tousled hair could attest.

"It's not that late, is it?" Zoey asked as she fished around her cluttered nightstand for her clock. It wasn't like Lucas to be concerned about the time while occupied in his favorite activity.

"No," Lucas replied, getting up from the bed, "but you have homework and I should let you do it."

"It's really not that much. You don't have to go, Lucas. I could do it on the ferry tomorrow," Zoey offered.

"That's okay, Zo," he responded, tucking his turtleneck back into his jeans. "You've had a long night. I should let you unwind."

"I am unwound," she said, rising to her knees to put her arms around his neck, "thanks to you."

"Anytime." Lucas kissed her lips briefly. "But I'm gonna take off. Good night," he said, giving her a final light kiss on the cheek.

"Good night," she responded as he crossed the room and headed out her bedroom door.

This wasn't the Lucas Cabral Zoey knew. That Lucas Cabral would never willingly end a make-out session. That Lucas Cabral had to be told when to stop. Zoey knew for certain that something was up. She just didn't know what.

Lucas let the cold water run across his face and down the length of his body. He tried to suppress a full-body shiver, but it was just no use. Cold showers definitely sucked.

But it had been worth it, he was convinced. As much as he wanted to stay with Zoey, he had vowed to himself that he wouldn't let things go too far. And he had stuck to his guns.

Throughout their relationship, the biggest source of conflict between Zoey and Lucas had been his desire— his sometimes overwhelming desire—to have sex.

Lucas knew that Zoey resented always having to be the one to cool things off. In fact, Lucas was sure that a big reason why Zoey had fooled around with that slimeball Aaron Mendel was that he'd fed her a line about wanting to remain a virgin.

No one will ever come between us again, Lucas thought as he lathered his arms. *I won't let it happen.* He'd adopted a new cool-off policy. From now on, before things got too heavy for Lucas to remain the polite, nonpressuring boyfriend he knew Zoey wanted, he would simply stop.

As difficult as it had been, he had done just that at Zoey's an hour before. She had seemed a little disappointed at first, but by the time he left, Lucas was sure he had detected a look of surprised happiness on Zoey's face.

Lucas heaved a sigh of satisfaction as he turned off the water. He was finally doing things the way Zoey had wanted all along. He would never come so close to losing her again.

He jumped in surprise as he heard a knock on the bathroom door. It was at least nine-thirty already. Because Mr. Cabral had to be up casting lobster nets by the crack of dawn, Lucas's parents were usually fast asleep by now. The only person who came by this late was Zoey, except for that one time Lara had tried to make a move on him . . . but she wouldn't pull that again, would she?

"Yeah?" Lucas called, wrapping a towel around himself for protection just in case.

"Lucas, dear, could I talk to you for a minute?" his mother's voice called from the other side of the door.

"Sure, just a second." Lucas knew something had to be up for her to still be awake. Besides, the Cabrals weren't exactly a family that took the time to chat with one another. In fact, he could probably count on his fingers the number of words he'd said to his mother in the past week.

Once he'd dried off enough to slip on his bathrobe, Lucas opened the door.

"Lucas," his mother said, "I'm sorry to disturb you, but I have some news I wanted you to know before tomorrow."

"What's up?" Lucas felt a momentary rush of concern and excitement. Maybe his parents were splitting up. Mr. Cabral had always been harsh toward his only son. He'd even wanted to send Lucas to relatives in Texas after Lucas had returned from the Youth Authority. Was his father going to be the one to leave now?

"Kate Levin is going to be moving in here tomorrow," Mrs. Cabral said.

"Kate Levin?" So much for divorce. Instead he was getting Kate Levin. His mom and Kate's mom were old friends from Holland, but Lucas hadn't seen Kate since he was ten years old and she was eleven.

His mother frowned. "I hadn't spoken to Anne in years, but she called this morning. It seems that Kate is studying at the New England Art Institute—photography, of all things."

"So she's going to live with us and take the ferry to Weymouth? For the next four years?"

"Oh, no, nothing like that. It's only going to be

8

temporary. The housing she had at school this semester fell through, so she'll just stay with us until they can find her another dormitory. I'm fixing up the spare room for her.''

''Great,'' Lucas said, his voice expressionless. Even if he hadn't seen her recently, Lucas knew that Kate, who had grown up in New York City, had always thought of him as a country hick.

''It could be a wonderful chance for you two to get reacquainted,'' Mrs. Cabral said, obviously not noticing her son's lack of excitement. ''You're so close in age. And Anne was my dearest playmate when I was a girl.''

''I know, Mom,'' Lucas responded, not wanting to stand in the hall and hear more reminiscences of Holland during World War II, when his grandparents hid their Jewish neighbors in their basement.

''Lucas,'' his mother said, finally detecting the note of unhappiness in his voice, ''you're not upset that Kate's coming, are you? I thought you'd like having someone your age in the house.''

''I'm not upset,'' he said. ''I don't really care. It's just that Kate and I have never exactly hit it off.''

Mrs. Cabral laughed, ''You haven't seen her since you were a little boy!''

''I know. It's just that she drank coffee—''

''She drank coffee? What does that have to do with anything?''

''She drank coffee and she thought it was funny that I'd never even tried it. She's always thought of me as a loser from the boonies.''

''Oh, Lucas,'' his mother said, pinching his cheek as though he were ten years old again, ''don't hold a silly grudge.''

Lucas shrugged. ''Whatever, Mom. It's fine with me

9

if she stays. Just don't expect us to be best friends."

"All I expect is that you show her some hospitality," his mother responded, turning away toward the stairs and her bedroom below. "Kate will be here tomorrow evening. And I hope that you two will get to know each other. That's all."

Just what I need, Lucas thought, *another person in this house who thinks I'm an idiot.*

Nina

Funny you should ask about love. It seems like my house has been bombed by Cupid.

First there was me and Benjamin. I guess to an outsider it may have been annoyingly sweet, but to me, becoming Benjamin's girlfriend was the most amazing thing that I'd ever experienced. I mean, here was this incredible guy who was smart, funny, gorgeous, the works, and whom I'd had a crush on since about the Ice Age. And suddenly he was into me. For real.

It gets lamer as the list goes on, though. The next thing I know, my dad brings home a woman to meet the family. Sarah Mendel is a perfectly nice woman, but she could have been a Munchkin from the Wizard of Oz. (I am referring here to both her size and her irritatingly happy demeanor.) Now Dad walks around with a dopey smile plastered on his face twenty-four hours a day, seven days a week. It's enough to warp a person's sense of reality.

But that's nothing compared to Aaron and the ice princess. Ever since the two of them got together, Claire has been bearing a striking resemblance to a human being. As if that weren't creepy enough, the guy is a few months away from being a member of our family. It's like step-incest!

But you didn't ask me who's in love—you asked me what love was.

Love is devotion. It's being there for someone through good or bad, thick or thin, rain or shine. It's the way I remember my parents being when my mother got sick.

That's how I know I really love Benjamin. The entire time he was recuperating from surgery, I wanted to be there to share it with him. The one thing I regret about the whole ordeal is that I let him talk me into coming home before his bandages came off. I should have been there the second

he realized he was still blind. Maybe
if I had shared that moment with
him, we would be closer now. I
don't know for sure.

Two

As usual, Nina Geiger poured way too much Cap'n Crunch into her bowl, leaving little room for the milk. *Why should anything go right today?* she thought as she poured the excess cereal back into the box. Ever since the morning, when she had overslept and had to run to catch the ferry, things had just not gone her way.

There was the American history pop quiz, on which she'd be lucky if she got a D. With everything else going on in Nina's life, studying had taken a burner even further back than usual. Even the two hours she'd put in that night trying to catch up hadn't been enough.

But academics weren't the worst of it. That day she'd made a whopping total of twelve funny remarks to Benjamin, and he hadn't laughed once.

Ever since he'd found out that the operation hadn't restored his sight, Benjamin had been in a funk. Which was normal; in fact, it would have been weird if he *hadn't* wanted to skip school and lie in bed all day, given the circumstances. But he'd been like this for a month now, and he showed no signs of snapping out of it anytime soon. No matter how disappointing it was to still be blind, he had to get on with his life, and Nina had been determined to cheer him up. But more and more she was realizing that her approach only seemed to make things worse.

In a way, Nina thought, it served her right. During the operation and the whole recovery period, she had been worried sick. But not about Benjamin. Nina had been afraid that when he was able to see, he'd be disappointed in, or even repulsed by her. She was afraid that if Benjamin were no longer blind, she'd lose him.

Nina had spent so much time trying to deal with her own anxieties, she hadn't really considered the possibility that the operation might fail. Somehow it had seemed too remote and painful a chance to worry about. Probably Benjamin had made the same assumptions she had. And it was still a huge shock for him.

She looked at the clock. Nine-thirty. She had told Benjamin she'd come by that night after she finished studying. It was getting kind of late, but Nina didn't want to let Benjamin down. The last thing he needed was another disappointment.

But would he even be disappointed if she didn't show up? Lately he hadn't seemed to care much whether or not she was there. Nina ate another spoonful of cereal.

"How can you say that?" her sister, Claire, exclaimed as she entered the kitchen, deep in conversation on the cordless phone. "John Malkovich is extremely sexy. Didn't you see *Dangerous Liaisons?*"

Claire listened intently to the other party as she crossed the kitchen and stuck a bag of popcorn into the microwave, running her fingers through her mane of black hair. Nina noted a slight spring in her sister's step. There was only one person who could be on the other end of the line—Aaron Mendel.

The Mendels were taking over Nina's house. Ever since Thanksgiving, the Geiger house had changed.

16

First her father, renowned for his emotionless, hermit-like behavior, was acting like a lovesick kid, and now her sister, the ice princess, was practically skipping through the kitchen. Nina was beginning to wonder if the other members of her family had been replaced by pod people.

"Well," Claire continued, "then the reason I think John Malkovich is sexy should be obvious to you. He's manipulative, conniving, and completely mesmerizing. Just my type." She sat down at the table next to Nina, suddenly aware of her sister's presence in the room. "Aaron, could you hold on a second?"

"Don't worry, Claire," Nina said quickly. "Your conversation's not interesting enough for me to listen to."

"I don't care if you're listening," Claire replied, covering the mouthpiece. "I'm just surprised that you're here. Weren't you going over to Benjamin's?"

"Don't worry, Claire. You'll be rid of me in a minute," Nina said, motioning to her nearly empty bowl of cereal.

Claire sighed. "Nina, I have no interest in getting rid of you. I just know how hard a time this is for Benjamin."

"So?" Nina asked, wondering where this was heading.

"So can't I be concerned? I don't think I have to remind you that Benjamin and I were close once."

No, Claire didn't have to remind Nina that she used to go out with Benjamin. In fact, a comment like that coming from her genetically blessed sister would once have rattled Nina. But not anymore. Not since Nina and Benjamin had shared something that he and Claire never had—sex.

"I don't know, Claire. *Can* you be concerned?"

Nina asked sarcastically. "I wasn't sure that was in the range of feeling of your species."

Claire let out another you're-so-immature-that-I'm-not-even-going-to-dignify-that-with-a-response sigh. "I just hope he's feeling better," she said, returning to the phone. "Sorry, Aaron, I just had to talk to Nina for a second. Anyway, do you now understand why I like John Malkovich? He reminds me of someone I know. . . ."

This is getting too gross, Nina thought.

"Intimately," Claire said.

Intimately? Had Claire and Aaron . . . *ewww!* He was going to be their stepbrother!

Claire actually giggled into the phone.

This was getting too weird for Nina, who got up, put her bowl in the sink, and headed to the closet to get her coat. No matter what kind of mood Benjamin was in, being with him had to be better than being with the newly lovey-dovey Claire.

"Have a good time, Nina," Claire called from the kitchen.

It almost sounded as if she meant it.

Benjamin ran his fingers across the CDs that lined the wall to the left of his bed. What to listen to that night? Chopin, Bach, Coltrane, the Gipsy Kings? Benjamin was having a hard time deciding as he touched the Braille labels. Zoey and Nina typed them up and stuck a label on the spine of each new disk in his collection so that he could tell which was which.

Braille. The code invented by a sighted person to give blind people the illusion that they could actually lead productive lives. Benjamin snorted ruefully. That was all it was—an illusion. His life would never be normal. As much as he liked to pretend otherwise, he would always be hopelessly dependent on others.

Even to listen to music he needed their help. Without labels, he would have no idea which CD he was taking from the rack. Without labels, he'd have no idea if he was hitting fast forward or pause on his stereo. And he'd always need someone to do the labeling. Always.

Benjamin sighed. He wanted music to drown out his thoughts. But all his music sounded empty and distant. Suddenly his fingers found a workable disk—Miles Davis's *Kind of Blue.*

I'm a little more than "kind of" blue, Benjamin thought as he placed the disk into his CD player and cranked up the volume. *But it's the same general idea.*

He eased back onto his bed as the sounds of jazz filled the space around him. Benjamin tapped his foot to the bass line of the first track, "So What."

So what? he thought. *So what? I'm blind. I've been blind for years now. So the operation didn't work—it was only a fifty-fifty chance to begin with. So what? Nothing is different. It's just a regular day.*

Everything was perfectly normal. He had heard Lucas leave a little while before. Soon afterward, he'd heard Zoey pacing the floor of the kitchen above him, looking for a snack. Occasionally he could hear the sound of a laugh track emanating from the TV his parents were watching in the den.

Just a normal night in the Passmore house. Everyone goes about their business, and the blind man listens and deciphers it all.

Benjamin rolled over in disgust. Zoey didn't spend her time figuring out if the footsteps in the hall belonged to Nina or Aisha. His parents didn't analyze every creak in the floorboards. That's because they could see. They had better things to do than wonder where every noise in the house came from.

As if in response to his thoughts, there was a knock on his door: two light taps followed by a thump. Nina.

"Come in," he called over the music.

"Hi." She sat down on the edge of his bed. "Mind if I turn down the music? Or are you going for a lounge lizard motif?"

"Go ahead," he said, ignoring a comment that was obviously meant to spark a smile. Benjamin wasn't in the mood to smile, not even for Nina. "Isn't it kind of late for you to be here?"

"It's almost ten. But I told you I'd stop by, and Nina Geiger, above all, is a woman of her word."

Great, now I'm a chore she has to take care of, Benjamin thought gloomily. *Better put in a visit to the blind boyfriend before bed*. His alliteration made Benjamin chuckle.

"What?" Nina asked, obviously eager to get in on the joke.

"Nothing," Benjamin said. "Just a stupid thought I had."

"I bet I can guess what kind of thought that was." Nina rubbed her hand on his leg suggestively. "It's been a while."

It *had* been a while. In the weeks before Benjamin had gotten his operation, he and Nina couldn't keep their hands off each other. But as the fateful day neared, Benjamin couldn't stay focused. And since the bandages came off, he had been too depressed. It had been well over a month since they had slept together.

But now wasn't the time to change that. Somehow Benjamin sensed that, as usual, Nina wanted to do something, anything, to cheer him up. And the last thing he wanted was for her to sleep with him out of pity.

He felt her lie down beside him and kiss his cheek, causing the right lens of his Ray-Bans to rise slightly. She started to run her fingers through his hair.

"Nina," Benjamin said, sitting up, "I don't think I'm in the mood for this right now."

"Okay," she said. "We can do whatever you want. Do you want me to start reading you *The Grand Inquisitor?*"

He could hear the forced cheerfulness in her tone. Benjamin knew she was straining to cover up her feelings of rejection—his rejection. He felt a pang of guilt. The last thing he wanted was to hurt Nina. But what else could he do? Pretending to want something he clearly didn't would be even worse.

"No, I don't think I want to start a new book yet."

"Okay," she said.

Okay! Okay! Everything was always okay! Couldn't she get it that nothing was okay? Benjamin knew that Nina was trying to help, but the effort in her voice only served to remind him of how bummed out he was. He knew she wanted him to be happy, which made him all the more depressed because he wasn't.

"Then why don't we lie here and listen to an opera?" Nina suggested. "Something passionate. Something depressing. Something in a foreign language that neither one of us understands."

Benjamin sighed. "I'm sorry, Nina," he said. "I don't really feel like it tonight."

"Well," Nina replied, obviously pretending to be unfazed, "what *do* you feel like doing? I'm up for anything you want."

"Well, if you don't mind—" he started.

"Of course I don't mind. Whatever you want," Nina interrupted, eager to please.

"I'd really like to be alone," Benjamin said.

As Nina said good night and left his room, Benjamin didn't need his sight to know she was disappointed.

Aisha

I used to think of love as the overwhelming desire to be with one person. Whenever you see them, it's like fireworks go off in your stomach or something, and you're so happy that you just don't want it to end. You want to be with that person more than anyone else in the world.

When you love someone, it's like the whole orbit of your life changes to include that person. It's not because you're weak or pathetic. It's because everything is just so much better when they're around.

I know that's the way it was for me and Christopher. Even though I have my friends and everything, I never felt truly complete, like I really belonged somewhere, until he came into my life. It had nothing to do with the black-white thing. It was more about being the new kid on the island. I had joined a group of friends who had known each other all their lives.

Don't get me wrong I really feel like part of the group now, and I did even before Christopher came along. But until him, I didn't have something that was truly mine, all mine.

If you had asked me about a month ago, I would have said that Christopher and I were in love. But even though my feelings for him are still the same, I don't know if I could say for sure now that we were, or are, in love.

Because if loving someone means you want to be with them more than anything else, why didn't I go with Christopher when he left Chatham Island to join the army? Why did I turn down his marriage proposal?

But then, if I didn't really love Christopher after all, why do I wish more than anything that he were still here?

Three

"Gross!" Aisha Gray exclaimed, spitting out the eraser she had accidentally chewed off her pencil.

She cursed herself as she tried to wipe off the acrid-tasting bits that were left on her tongue. Maybe biting off the eraser would teach her to stay focused on the physics she was supposed to be studying. Instead Aisha had been zoning out for the past half hour, thinking about Christopher Shupe.

What was he doing right at that moment? He was probably asleep in some barrack, pulling a scratchy wool blanket up to his chin to keep warm. Although she didn't know for sure what kind of bed he had, Aisha always pictured Christopher on the bottom bunk in a room that looked like something out of that old TV show *M*A*S*H*. Because of this mental image, she had to constantly remind herself that Christopher was just in the army—not in an actual war.

But it was hard to do that when she felt as though he were a world away. When she'd received only one short postcard from him since he'd left, exactly a month before.

Even the postcard had done nothing to help Aisha picture what Christopher's new life was like. But it was something concrete to hold on to. For the fifth time that hour, Aisha opened the top drawer of her desk and pulled out the card. Though she'd received it only a week earlier, the edges were already starting to fray. Aisha stared down at the card and read the same words she'd read a thousand times before:

January 25

Aisha,

Just dropping you this note to let you know I made it here in one piece. Things here are okay. Up early, asleep early, and the food is terrible, but not as bad as I thought. Tell everyone I say hi, especially your family.

I'll put my address on the bottom in case you ever want to write.

Take care,
Christopher

Every time she read the postcard, Aisha was struck by the same thing. He hadn't even written *Dear Aisha*. It could mean only one thing: that as much as Aisha had explained that it had nothing to do with her feelings for him, Christopher was definitely still angry at her for turning down his marriage proposal.

She had thought he'd understand her decision in time, maybe even come to agree with her. They were just too young to make a commitment that would have to last the rest of their lives. But it was obvious from his cold, impersonal postcard that Christopher didn't feel the same way.

In fact, Aisha couldn't be sure what feelings, if any, Christopher had for her now.

I can't think about this, she scolded herself. *I have work to do.*

Aisha threw the postcard down on her open physics textbook, determined to get back to her reading. But the final line of the postcard caught her eye: *I'll put my address on the bottom in case you ever want to write.*

Should she write to him or not? Zoey had said she should, reasoning that Christopher wouldn't have included the address if he didn't want to hear from Aisha. Besides, he had loved Aisha enough to want to marry her, so of course he'd want to get a letter from her. But that was Zoey, Chatham Island's biggest sap.

Claire had told her not to write. What was the point? Christopher wanted a clean break, and after you turn down someone's offer of marriage, what else is there to say? But that was Claire, the ice princess.

Nina had been no help. She was even more indecisive than Aisha.

What Aisha needed was a guy's opinion. But Benjamin was hardly in any shape to help her out. And Lucas had just shrugged and said it was none of his business. Guys could be so annoying.

Finally Aisha picked up her pen and found a clean sheet of paper in her spiral notebook. She might as well write a letter. It didn't mean she had to send it.

Wednesday February 5th
Dear Christopher

Yes, she would put *dear.*

Dear Christopher,
I got your postcard last week. It was so good to hear from you. I'm glad the

food is better than you thought. What is it like in the army? It's so hard for me to imagine.

Things on Chatham Island are the same. Zoey and Lucas are tighter than ever. Benjamin is still really depressed because his operation didn't work, and

Aisha stared at the page. What was she, the town gossip? Why was she writing to Christopher about everyone else on the island? All she wanted to do was let him know she still cared. She tore out the page, crumpled it up, and threw it into the trash.

She stared at the new, blank piece of paper, determined to start again.

"Take two," she said, bracing her pen.

Feb. 5

Dear Christopher,

I was so happy to get your postcard last week. I'm glad things there are okay. I'd love to hear more about them if you have the time to write.

Things on Chatham Island are pretty much same old, same old. Except that everyone misses you. Especially me.

I don't know where things stand with us now, but I really hope that you

*can find it in your heart to forgive me.
I know I told you this before, but I
didn't say no to you because of the way
I felt about you. I said no because
we're just too young.*

*I will never forget how happy you
made me the night you asked me to be
your wife. It was probably the best
night of my life.*

Aisha had to stop writing as the tears welled up in
her eyes. She wiped them away and reread what she'd
written so far. *I will never forget . . .* why did it sound
so final? So in the past? Her feelings for Christopher
weren't over. Why did their relationship have to be?

She looked back at his postcard. He couldn't forgive
her. Not yet, not ever. Claire was right—what was
there to say?

"*That's* why it's over." Aisha threw her second at-
tempt at a letter into the trash.

*I just have to accept that Christopher and I are his-
tory*, she thought as she turned back to her physics
notes. *The sooner the better.*

Claire Geiger stood on her widow's walk hugging
her chenille blanket around her for some warmth. It
was a cold, crisp February night, and Claire loved the
sting the chilly air gave to the tip of her nose. It felt
like a pinch that let her know she wasn't dreaming.

The night was cold, but the cloudless sky showed
no storm in sight. It was so clear that Claire could see
the constellations in the winter sky—the Big Dipper,

Orion the hunter, and her favorite, Cassiopeia the queen.

Claire's thoughts were interrupted by the sound of footsteps on the ground below her. Who would be out walking around at that time of night? It had to be eleven o'clock. Maybe her dad was having prewedding jitters. She stood up and leaned over the railing to get a better look. Pacing in the cold winter air, an unlit cigarette dangling from her lips, was her sister, Nina.

Something must have happened at Benjamin's, Claire realized as she leaned back.

Claire knew that Benjamin was going through a lot. She also knew that, like her, Benjamin didn't feel comfortable talking about his pain with anyone, not even the people closest to him. Especially not the people closest to him.

It had been a kind of bond between them. In fact, Claire sometimes thought that it was the only thing that had made their relationship work. They each knew instinctively not to get too close. But now Benjamin was with Nina.

Claire pulled the blanket tighter around her shoulders. She could hear Nina continuing to pace the front yard, and she felt a surge of protective love for her younger sister. The rush of emotion surprised her.

She was feeling everything more warmly, more immediately lately, and Claire knew who was responsible for that. The corners of her mouth lifted into a grin as she thought of the difference Aaron Mendel had made in her life.

For the first time since her mother had died, Claire felt truly happy. She could finally let down her guard and be loved for who she was. What was the point of keeping up that guard when Aaron could see right through it, anyway?

Claire sighed contentedly as she reached behind the brick that held her journal. Sitting back down, she opened the small book to the next blank page, uncapped her pen, and started to write.

February 5th

19 degrees. Winds minimal. Sky clear and cloudless. No precipitation anticipated.

Claire looked up, thinking about what to write. She had never been blocked while writing in her journal before. In a way, her journal had been Claire's best friend—the only place where she could bare her soul, reveal her schemes, tell the whole truth, and actually relax.

Again she smiled. *Now I have Aaron for that*, she thought. She turned again to the nearly blank page and wrote a single sentence.

I love Aaron.

Four

The air on the sheltered lower level of the *Island Breeze* was thick and stuffy, but it was way too cold to stay on the upper deck.

"It's a no-win situation," Nina said. "Either we stay upstairs and get pneumonia or we huddle together down here and breathe in each other's recycled germs."

Aisha shrugged. "Add that to the list of things in our lives that suck," she said.

"At least I'm not the only one in a bad mood this morning," Nina said as Aisha continued to stare out into space.

Nina swung her feet, knocking her combat boots against the wall of the cabin. She, Claire, Aisha, and Jake had already boarded the boat, but the rest of the island crowd had yet to arrive. She looked at her watch. 7:41. Lucas, Zoey, and, most important, Benjamin still had four minutes to get there.

Benjamin. Ever since she'd left his room the night before, Nina hadn't been able to think straight. She had paced around her house like a crazy woman and stayed up late watching Letterman and even part of Conan O'Brien.

Benjamin wasn't mad at *her*—he was just mad,

Nina had reasoned to herself. And he had a right to be. The failure to regain his sight had been a big disappointment. But why was he shutting her out?

Their whole relationship had been a dream come true for Nina. For years she had secretly wanted Benjamin, but he'd been dating supermodel Claire. Even after she and Benjamin had become a couple, Nina was always afraid that one day Benjamin would realize he could have any girl he wanted and give her the heave-ho. Maybe spending all that time alone in the hospital had finally led him to exactly that conclusion.

Of course, it was possible that Benjamin had just happened to be in the mood for solitude. There was no crime in that. He was entitled to some space. Maybe he wasn't pushing her away at all.

I have to see him to make sure he's not mad at me.

To make matters worse, Claire had asked Nina at breakfast that morning if everything was okay. Her voice had sounded so genuine, it was creepy. Nina glanced toward the other side of the boat, where her sister sat calmly reading the paper. Claire was probably just trying to rattle her. Unfortunately, it had worked.

Nina took the last Lucky Strike from the pack and stuck it in her mouth. *If this keeps up, I may start lighting them*, she thought as she sucked in the sweet tobacco taste. She stared out the window in front of her.

The departure whistle blew.

"Hi, guys," Zoey said, trying to catch her breath.

"Thank God you're here," Nina said, her face breaking into a smile of relief. "I was beginning to think you guys were going to have to shell out the bucks for the water taxi."

The smile quickly faded. Zoey and Lucas were out

of breath from their last-second arrival. But Benjamin was not with them.

"Benjamin decided not to come to school today," Zoey said, skipping the usual greetings.

"Yeah," Lucas chimed in, "about ten minutes ago."

"We were trying to convince him to get out of the house. That's why we were late," Zoey explained.

"Did he say why?" Nina asked. "I mean, is he sick or anything?"

"He said he just wasn't in the mood," Lucas told her. "I was like, who is?"

"He was all dressed and everything, and then he just got up from breakfast and announced that he wasn't coming." Zoey sighed.

Nina tried to remain calm, but her restless night was getting the better of her. "Zoey, I know this is going to sound really stupid, but he didn't say anything about me, did he?"

"About you? No. Like what?"

"Like that he didn't want to see me or something?"

"Of course not! Benjamin loves you!" Zoey exclaimed.

"I wish I didn't need you to keep reminding me of that fact," Nina replied shakily.

"He's just not ready to get back to normal yet. That's all."

"I know." Nina felt the tears welling up in her eyes. "But I just don't know what to do. I'm trying hard to be understanding and everything. I even offered to listen to opera—"

"That *is* understanding," Lucas said.

"—but he just wants to be alone," Nina finished, wiping away the tears that were now falling down her cheek.

Zoey put a comforting arm around Nina's shoulder. "Nina, you're not the only one he's treating like this. He leaves his room only for meals, and even then he barely says a word to anyone."

"I just don't know what to do, Zoey." Nina took in a quick breath and then let it out in an exasperated sigh.

"We all just have to give him some space," Zoey said. "It's something he has to work out on his own. You know Benjamin—he always bounces back. But I guess he needs more time to accept this."

"So what do I do in the meantime?" Nina asked. "I'm no good at being the strong, silent type."

"Just do what the rest of us are doing," Zoey suggested. "Be normal. It will make it that much easier for Benjamin to get back to normal, too."

Nina sighed. "Normal isn't my strong suit, either." She crushed her now soggy cigarette in the palm of her hand.

Zoey giggled. "Normal for *you*, Nina. Even you can manage that."

Jake McRoyan sat on the uncomfortable ferry bench trying to make his way through act two of *Macbeth*. He had to read the play and write a paper on it, even though the assignment was for extra credit. As it stood now, his grade in English was barely a D, which was good enough to pass but not good enough for him to start on the baseball team. If he didn't raise his grade to at least a C, Jake could kiss the spring season good-bye.

That which has made them drunk hath made me bold;

> What hath quenched them hath given
> me fire. Hark! Peace!

Even in Shakespeare's time, people were getting wasted and screwing up their lives—just what Jake had done to get himself roped into writing this paper. If he hadn't turned his *Scarlet Letter* paper in two weeks late and hadn't skipped studying for his final because of a drunken binge with Lara, he wouldn't be stuck reading this play.

But all of that was in the past. Jake had finally turned over a new leaf; he'd gotten himself into AA and on the right track. And even if Louise Kronenberger had her doubts, Jake hoped that Lara was clean now, too.

What he didn't know was where things stood between him and Lara. He had vowed to end the relationship over Christmas break, when Lara had spent the night in a drunken stupor cursing out both Jake and Lucas while she threw up all over Jake's bathroom.

But since her father had made her move out, Lara hadn't touched a drop of alcohol. And she had painted a portrait of Jake that was probably the nicest thing anyone had ever done for him. Part of Jake knew that Lara's thank-you had been a way to get him back in her life. Still, he worried about her, and he did want to help. Maybe eventually Lara would change her mind about AA, which she said was "too touchy-feely," and he'd be able to persuade her to join.

Not fooling around with Lara had been one of Jake's New Year's resolutions, and Jake had held out for a good two weeks, just to make sure that Lara was really serious about not drinking. So what was the harm in seeing a totally attractive girl who was totally into him, as long as she was totally clean?

"*Macbeth*, huh?"

Jake was suddenly aware that someone had sat down beside him. He looked up from his book and was surprised to see Aisha Gray looking at him intently.

"Yeah," Jake replied.

His surprise must have been obvious. "Look, Jake," Aisha started, "I know you're probably thinking, 'Why is this girl talking to me?' "

"Hey," he said with a shrug, "it's a small ferry."

"True. But you and I aren't exactly . . . close."

Aisha and he traveled in the same circles. They had hung out together fairly often in a large group, especially when Jake had been with Zoey. But Jake couldn't remember ever actually having held a one-on-one conversation with Aisha.

It wasn't that they didn't like each other. It was just that Jake McRoyan and Aisha Gray had never really had anything to say to each other.

"Yeah, I guess not," Jake replied, unsure where this was heading.

"It's just that, well, I kind of need a guy's opinion on something, but Lucas doesn't want to butt in, and Benjamin has enough to deal with as it is, so—"

"So that leaves me," Jake said, completing Aisha's sentence for her.

"Right. I mean, if you don't mind. Or if you're not too busy," she said, gesturing toward his book. "I mean, you don't have to or anything."

What could she possibly want to ask him? If she wanted a guy's opinion, it probably had something to do with Christopher Shupe. Jake knew that things had been pretty serious between Aisha and Christopher before he left. Whatever it was, her discomfort stirred Jake's curiosity. It had to be better than reading *Macbeth*. He closed the book and put it down next to him. "What's up?"

Aisha sighed. "Well, I don't know if you know or not, but Christopher enlisted in the army."

Even if Christopher hadn't told Jake that himself, Jake would still have known that piece of news, because Lara had moved out of the Passmores' house and into Christopher's old apartment. And because they lived on a tiny island where news—good or bad—traveled like wildfire. *What does she think I am, some dumb jock who has no idea what's going on around him*? "Yeah, I knew that," Jake said.

"Well, he asked me to marry him before he left, and I said no."

Jake knew about this, too, but decided to remain silent.

"It had nothing to do with how I felt about him," Aisha continued, picking up steam. "It was just too soon. I mean, I would have had to move away from my family and my friends and start this whole new life. Not to mention figure out what to do about college. I just thought we were too young for all that."

Jake nodded. "Well, it is a big commitment."

"Right. So you understand that? I mean, that makes sense to you?"

What was this, some kind of pop quiz? "It's pretty straightforward."

"But not to Christopher. I mean, I explained all of this to him, but he's still mad at me. And what I was wondering is, from a guy's perspective, should I try to write to him and explain it again? To, you know, work things out?"

Just as Jake had suspected, she wanted some love

advice. Aisha didn't think Jake was an idiot at all. In fact, she probably had no idea what a mess he had managed to make of his own love life in recent memory. First Zoey, then Claire, then a drunken one-night stand with Louise, and now Lara. Only Lara wasn't really a mistake. At least he didn't think so.

"I don't know, Aisha," Jake answered. "It sounds like Christopher already knows the score, but he's just not happy with it."

"So what does that mean? Should I write him or not?"

"Look, Aisha. Asking someone to marry you is a huge deal, army or not. Even if you didn't want to break up with him, you still gave Christopher a pretty big rejection."

"But I wasn't rejecting *him*. I was rejecting *marriage*."

"That's the way you see it. But to Christopher, the two are the same thing."

She looked really bummed out. "So what should I do?"

"Sometimes you just need to walk away. Forget the past and move on."

"So I shouldn't write him, then."

Jake heard a laugh from the other end of the ferry. He didn't need to look behind him to know it came from Zoey.

"As hard as it is, Aisha," he said, "sometimes you just have to make a clean break. When it's over, it's over."

Five

Zoey looked up at the blackboard. It was getting more and more difficult to pay attention in French class. Mme. Eisler was droning on and on about the pluperfect, a verb tense whose purpose Zoey couldn't figure out for the life of her. Maybe Nina had been right: She should have gone the easy route and taken Spanish.

But then she wouldn't be able to sit next to Lucas in class. Zoey sneaked a glance in her boyfriend's direction. He looked just as lost as she was, and maybe even a bit more bored.

What is Lucas thinking?

It was a question she'd been asking herself since the night before, when Lucas had left her room in the middle of fooling around. She couldn't understand it. Unless he hadn't really forgiven her for her stupid attraction to Aaron Mendel. Or, more important, for acting on it.

As inconspicuously as possible, she turned her spiral notebook to a clean sheet of paper.

Lucas,
This is so boring! I keep

*spacing out. In another
minute I'm going to fall
asleep. Write back.*

Zoey signed her name, proud of her casual approach. Now the only problem was passing her note. If she tried to rip the paper out of her notebook, it would make too much noise. The classroom was nearly silent. You could hear people breathing.

No, she'd have to wait until Mme. Eisler went to write on the board. Once the teacher's back was turned, Zoey would slide the whole notebook onto Lucas's desk. Since they were sitting side by side in the fourth row, the teacher would never notice.

Almost as if on command, Mme. Eisler turned to the blackboard. But Lucas's elbow was in the way. Zoey tapped him on the arm and handed him her notebook. It wasn't covert, but it got the job done.

Lucas scribbled something back, and the two of them exchanged sneaky glances. It was very eighth-grade to pass notes in class, but it was still fun.

When Mme. Eisler turned to the board again, Lucas handed the notebook back to Zoey. Zoey eagerly read his response.

*Zoey,
I bet I'm more bored
than you are. And we still
have 25 minutes left.*

Benjamin had the right
idea. We should all skip
school more often.

Meanwhile, try watching
Mme. Eisler's mole. It
always keeps me awake.

LUCAS

Zoey had to suppress a giggle. It was hard not to notice the big mole on Mme. Eisler's cheek. At least it wasn't a hairy one; if it had been, nobody would ever stay focused on French.

She wrote back:

Lucas,
The mole is helpful, but only a little. Instead I've decided to think about my after-school plans. I think Aisha and I are going to the mall. She's really bummed out about Christopher. I think some shopping will help cheer her up. Will you come? We won't try on clothes the whole time, I promise.

Please?

Write back.
Zoey

When Mme. Eisler looked down at her textbook, Zoey handed her notebook to Lucas again. If they got caught and Mme. Eisler read the note, it would be not only embarrassing but also, thanks to the mole discussion, potentially harmful to their grades.

Zoey allowed herself to look in Lucas's direction. He was still writing, fast and furiously. A few minutes later the notebook was back on her desk.

Zoey,
You two can't control yourselves. There's no way I wouldn't spend the whole trip waiting around for you guys. But I can't go anyway.

I forgot to tell you this morning because of the whole Benjamin thing, but this girl, Kate Levin, is coming to stay at my house for a while.

Do you remember how I told you that my mother's parents hid their neighbors in their basement? You know, because the Nazis invaded Holland And the people who lived next door were Jewish? Well, Anne (the neighbor's daughter) And my mom were really good friends. Anne lives in New York, but her daughter Kate just started at the New England Art Institute. Photography, I think my mom said. Anyway, something happened with Kate's dorm, so she's staying with us until it gets cleared

44

up. My mom told me last night that Kate's coming today, so I have to go home and help out or something.

Have a good time without me.

                              Lucas

Zoey looked up from her notebook. Someone was coming to live with the Cabrals? She flashed Lucas a look of confusion. He shrugged back at her, acknowledging that it was indeed a little weird.

Zoey quickly dashed a note back.

What is Kate like?

This time she handed Lucas the notebook without waiting for a move from Mme. Eisler. There were less than five minutes left in the period, anyway.

Lucas responded and returned the notebook to Zoey with a similar lack of caution.

I don't really know. The last time I saw her, she was eleven and I was ten.

Zoey thought for a moment and then wrote:

Was she pretty?

"Zoey, qu'est-ce tu fais?" Mme. Eisler's nasal

voice rang out across the classroom. Everyone turned to look at Zoey, whose arm was outstretched incriminatingly. In her hand was the telltale notebook.

"Nothing," Zoey said. She could feel the flush rising to her cheeks.

Mme. Eisler glared. "I hope it was nothing," she said menacingly before resuming her lecture. A moment later her fellow classmates turned back around. Zoey had been lucky to get off with a reprimand.

She turned to Lucas, who mouthed the words "I'm sorry."

I guess I'll have to wait to find out all about Kate Levin, she thought. And about *Lucas's sudden disinterest in sex*.

"Hey, Nina, wait up," Aisha called down the crowded hallway. She could see Nina stop in her tracks and turn around to look for her friend.

"Where's the fire?" Nina asked.

"At the mall," Aisha replied. "Zoey and I are going after school. Want to come?"

Nina shook her head. "No, thanks," she said. "I think I'm going to see Benjamin."

Aisha should have known. She felt a pang of guilt. She'd been so wrapped up in her thoughts about Christopher that morning that she hadn't really been paying attention to Nina. And since she'd been finishing her physics homework in the library during lunch, Aisha hadn't had a chance to talk to Nina then, either. Some friend she was.

"Yeah, that's probably a good thing," Aisha said, trying to be supportive.

Nina rolled her eyes. "I hope."

"You know, the only reason Zoey and I are going is to cheer me up," Aisha said. "But I'm starting to think that you're the one who needs a shopping spree.''

''Maybe some other time, Eesh,'' Nina said as she turned the corner. ''But thanks for the offer.''

''Tell Benjamin I said hi,'' Aisha called as her friend headed off to class.

Aisha thought back to the day she had first helped Benjamin go online. When the two of them had discovered that doctors at Boston General were working on restoring sight to people like Benjamin, he had sworn Aisha to secrecy. She'd gone along with it, but she hadn't really understood his desire for secrecy.

Now she did. He hadn't wanted to get their hopes up, even though his had probably already been soaring. Benjamin had wanted to spare the people around him the kind of grief he was going through now. Aisha wished there were something she could do for him.

For the millionth time that day she wished she could talk to Christopher. She was used to talking everything over with him.

Aisha felt a cool hand on her shoulder.

''Aisha Gray, I've been looking all over for you!'' One of the guidance counselors, Mrs. Homes, stared down at her through half-rimmed glasses. The glasses, combined with her long graying hair and tie-dyed skirt, reminded Aisha that the sixties were a long, long time ago.

''Hi, Mrs. Homes,'' she said.

Unlike some of her fellow students, Aisha wasn't exactly the pour-your-heart-out-to-the-guidance-counselor-just-to-get-out-of-class type. In fact, the longest amount of time she'd spent in the guidance office had been about ten minutes.

''What's up?'' Aisha asked, hoping nothing was wrong with her college recommendations.

"I have some absolutely wonderful news," Mrs. Homes chirped, all three of her chins flapping. "You are a finalist for the Westinghouse science scholarship! Isn't that terrific?"

"The Westinghouse scholarship?" Aisha had no idea what Mrs. Homes was talking about.

"Yes," the counselor answered. "It's awarded every year to the top senior in science, and you have a very good shot at getting it."

"Wow," Aisha said. She had barely gotten her physics problem sent in on time. "Is there anything I have to do?"

"All you have to do is keep up the studying. The science department will make its determination at the end of March, so just keep up the good work until then!"

"I will," Aisha said, feeling her eyes widen in amazement. "Thanks for telling me, Mrs. Homes."

"Oh, it was my pleasure," she replied, squeezing Aisha's shoulder as she turned off in the other direction. "You've got a great shot at this, Aisha. And if you get it, you can count on getting into almost any college you want."

For the first time in a while, Aisha wanted to jump for joy. Science had always been her best subject, but she'd had no idea she was at the top of her class. The best student in science. The scholarship. Getting into any college she wanted.

Suddenly Aisha didn't need shopping to cheer her up.

But she was only a finalist, she reminded herself. She still had almost two months to go before she would know whether or not she'd won. Two months of working her hardest to ace every physics homework assignment, quiz, and test. Two months of not allowing any distractions.

Distractions such as thinking about Christopher.

Six

Sprawled out on his couch, Benjamin reached for the coffee table. He felt around for the bag of microwave popcorn he'd heated up an hour before, hoping not to misjudge the distance and spill its contents all over the floor.

A few feet away, dinosaurs were roaring. At least Benjamin thought they were dinosaurs. *Jurassic Park* was in the VCR, and he'd heard a lot of talk about tyrannosauruses, but Benjamin couldn't be sure that the loud cries that blasted out of the TV were really supposed to belong to prehistoric beasts of any kind.

"Hi," called a voice from the back of the room.

Nina had caught him off guard. Benjamin wished he could remember what he'd done with the remote control. The volume was up so loud, he hadn't even heard Nina enter the house.

"How's it going?" Nina leaned in to peck his cheek, and Benjamin was distracted by the smell of her shampoo. Peaches.

This was what he'd be reduced to forever: identifying his girlfriend by the smell of some hair product. Next thing he knew, Benjamin would be like a dog, sniffing everyone's crotch for identification.

"Blind as ever," he said.

One thing about still being blind, he thought, *is that I can still savor the awkward silences*.

After about a minute she spoke again. "Well, you missed another action-packed Thursday at Weymouth High. The macaroni and cheese had its usual beige hue and tasted like a combination of cardboard and slugs. And I got back my American history pop quiz. A sixty-one. The sad thing is, I was psyched."

Benjamin gave a sympathetic snort. Nina wasn't the only one whose grades were in the toilet.

"Oh, yeah, and some girl's moving in with the Cabrals," Nina added. "Some friend of the family."

Great, thought Benjamin, *another set of footsteps to memorize*.

"In other words, you didn't miss much," she told him.

"What a surprise."

"*Jurassic Park*, huh? I never pegged you for a Spielberg fan." Nina must have finally noticed the movie.

"Yeah, well, he sees the world through the eyes of a child," Benjamin quipped. "Which is more than I can say for myself."

He heard Nina sigh and felt the couch cushions shift. She must have been leaning over, examining the titles of the other movies his mother had rented for him: *Timecop, Terminator 2—Judgment Day*, and *Aliens*. Bingeing on almost-plotless special-effects movies seemed an appropriate way to nurse his blues. Half the time he had no clue what was even going on in the films.

"Interesting selection," Nina said. "Which ones have you watched?"

"To tell you the truth, I really don't know," he lied. Mrs. Passmore had just brought the movies home, and

Benjamin hadn't watched any of them yet. Instead he had spent the afternoon listening to soap operas and wishing that he were in a coma like someone named Tad.

"Well, why don't we watch one together? I'll fill you in on the extraviolent parts," Nina offered.

"That would kind of defeat my purpose," Benjamin responded.

Again there was silence. Benjamin could almost feel the dead air between them. Why was he doing this to her? All she wanted was to help.

"You know what you could do for me, though?" he asked.

"What?" Nina answered eagerly.

"You could find me something to drink."

He felt her spring up from the couch. "Sure. What do you want? Dr Pepper?"

"No," Benjamin replied. "I could get that myself. Something alcoholic."

Benjamin had never had any particular desire to drink before, but now seemed like the perfect time to start. Maybe some inebriation would take his mind off everything else. Since he had no idea where his parents kept the liquor, this was yet another thing he couldn't do on his own. Knowing his luck, he'd pass out on the floor from drinking Pine Sol.

"What?" Benjamin could hear the surprise in Nina's voice.

"I want a real drink."

"I don't know if that's such a good idea, Benjamin."

"Don't get all parental on me, Nina," he said. "After all, I am nineteen years old. In case you've forgotten."

"I haven't forgotten and I'm not being parental. I

just don't think getting drunk is going to make you feel any better.''

"And just how do you know what's going to make me feel better, Nina? Maybe nothing will, so maybe I should just get loaded.''

"This isn't you, Benjamin. You sound like Lara or something.''

Benjamin knew Nina was bringing up his semidelinquent half sister to make him change his mind. "Well, it could run in the family,'' he said.

"Benjamin.'' Nina took his hand. "You don't need to drink. And you don't need to do this alone. Why don't you just talk to me instead? I want to help you get through this.''

Her voice was shaking with emotion, and Benjamin suddenly yearned to comfort her, to let her comfort him.

"Please, Benjamin,'' Nina said softly. "I can't stand to see you like this.''

What must he look like to her, he wondered, lying there on the couch with his smudged Ray-Ban sunglasses and unwashed hair? He hadn't showered in days. Was it pity she was feeling?

He snatched back his hand. "If you want to help me, go get me some booze. If not, you may as well leave.''

He listened as Nina's footsteps ran quickly out the door.

Nina had spent the last twenty minutes in the air. She hadn't jumped on her bed since she was about ten years old, but all of a sudden she had needed to relieve her stress. She sat down in exhaustion and felt her head begin to throb.

Maybe she should turn down the music. As soon as

she had returned home from that awful scene with Benjamin, she had blasted Nirvana as loud as her stereo would allow. Like Benjamin, Kurt Cobain had been depressed and angry. Unfortunately, he had wound up with a gun in his mouth.

Maybe Nirvana wasn't such a great choice after all, Nina thought as she pressed the stop button.

She rolled back over and lay down, sprawled out across her bed, which was now a total mess. Nina stared up at the ceiling and tried unsuccessfully to think about something other than Benjamin.

Had she been wrong to leave? She hadn't wanted to get Benjamin a drink. Even if she had felt comfortable sneaking around the Passmores' kitchen searching for the goods, Nina didn't think drinking was a good idea for Benjamin just then. Acting stupid, singing off key, and throwing up on himself would not exactly tear him out of his funk.

But what would? Nina had tried her best to help him, but so far nothing had even come close to working. In fact, she was beginning to suspect that Benjamin dreaded her presence. Maybe Zoey was right and Benjamin didn't want to talk to anybody just then, but Nina wasn't just anybody. They were a couple. They were supposed to be in love.

Nina rose from her bed and began pacing her carpeted floor. There had to be something she could do, someone she could talk to. Nina glanced at the clock. 4:15. Things wouldn't be too hectic at Passmores' now; they were probably just getting things ready for the dinner shift.

Time for another heart-to-heart with Mrs. P., Nina thought as she headed out her bedroom door. Why not talk to Benjamin's mom about it? It wasn't nearly as humiliating as talking to her about Nina and Benjamin's sex life had been.

Nina opened the front door to leave and practically ran into Claire, who was too busy examining the mail to look where she was going.

"Where are you off to in such a hurry?" Claire asked, arching one of her perfectly tweezed eyebrows. "To Benjamin's?"

"No, Claire, I was already there. I have to go see someone. It's kind of important, so if you don't mind getting out of the way—"

"I will in a second," Claire interrupted, still blocking Nina's path, "but I want to say something to you first."

Nina rolled her eyes. "Claire, please don't cast a spell on me today. I have other things on my mind."

"I know you do, and that's what I want to talk to you about."

Claire looked deadly serious. She had even let the spell remark pass without so much as a bored snort. Nina looked into her sister's eyes. On anyone but Claire, Nina would have thought she recognized an expression of concern.

"What?" Nina tried to sound bored rather than bewildered.

"Look, Nina," Claire began, "I know that Benjamin's been depressed. I know that he's been skipping school—which is totally out of character. And I know that every time you come back from his house you either blast music or pace around in the freezing cold."

"I had no idea you were keeping tabs on me, Claire. I'm touched."

"You can be as sarcastic as you want, Nina. I really

don't care. All I know is that you're upset. And I know we aren't exactly best friends—"

"Right again."

"—but I want you to know that if you ever want to talk, I'm here for you."

"Thanks, I think," Nina replied, unable this time to conceal her bafflement.

"I'm serious, Nina," Claire said, entering the house and clearing the way for Nina to leave. "Anytime."

There for her? Claire? Nina paused for a second, thoroughly confused. Could Claire actually be using her powers for good instead of evil?

Nina shook off the thought as she headed down the porch steps. She couldn't afford to get sidetracked by Claire's sudden quasi compassion. She had to figure out what to do about Benjamin.

Seven

Claire climbed the steps to her room feeling very pleased with herself. Rather than reveling in the selfish joy of receiving a letter from Aaron, Claire had focused her energies on her sister's problems. It had felt nice to reach out to Nina, even if Nina hadn't yet realized how grateful she would be to Claire.

Now that she'd accomplished her good deed for the day, Claire hurried to her room, excited to open Aaron's letter and savor every word. It dawned on her that this was the first actual love letter that she had ever received.

Lucas and Jake weren't exactly the kind of guys who expressed themselves in prose, and Claire's whole relationship with Benjamin had been about avoiding self-expression. The closest Claire had come to love notes was her short-lived Internet relationship with a guy named Flyer, but that had come to a screeching halt once the two met face-to-face.

As she shut her bedroom door Claire decided that her correspondence with Flyer didn't count. After all, they had never really been a couple, only a potential couple. Nothing like what she and Aaron were to each other.

Claire took off her coat and made herself comfortable on the bed. She wanted to take her time, keep her cool. She had been fighting off the impulse to rip the letter open and devour it right away. When she read it, she would be calm and collected.

She took a deep breath and, with a smile on her lips, tore the envelope open and pulled out its contents. Lying on her stomach, she began to read.

February 3—12:30 A.M.

Dear Claire,

Another late night of studying. Who said second semester senior year was a blow off?

I wish I could call you to say good night, but I doubt Burke would take too kindly to a call from his future stepson at 12:30 at night. Besides, you're probably fast asleep already.

Or maybe you're on your widow's walk, huddled under your blanket with your hair flying around in the wind. The bewitching girl casting her spell on her little island, surveying it all from her favorite perch. I wish I were there with you, looking up at the winter sky, hatching plans to make mischief on the poor, unsuspecting souls below. Or even just keeping you warm on a cold winter's night.

But I'm not there, am I? I'm in my lonely little dorm room, which is unbearably hot (that's the thing with charming old buildings, you can never control the heat) and characteristically untidy. And all I have to remind me of the mysterious girl from that cold Maine island is one lousy picture. Of course, it can't do her justice. But I do have memories, which for now will have to do the trick.

I was hoping that writing this might make me tired, but thinking about you has done nothing but make me more alert. Even miles away, you still keep me on my toes, Claire.

I was going to tell you this on the phone tomorrow, but now I'm thinking it may be more fun to write it here as a surprise. A girl from another boarding school is throwing a big party in Portland on Valentine's Day. A bunch of people from here are going, which means I can hitch a ride fairly easily. But only if you'll meet me there. That way we can be together on Valentine's Day.

Please come, Claire. I don't know about you, but I've never had anyone I really wanted to be with on Valentine's Day before. We can ditch the party and do something else together, just the two of us. I know you'll find a convenient way to convince Burke to give you the car. After all, it's for the sake of our cozy new family, right?

I'm going to sign off now, Claire, to either work on your Valentine's Day present (yes, you're getting one) or see you in my dreams.

Love,
Aaron

As she folded the letter Claire let out a sigh of satisfaction. Valentine's Day with Aaron. Of course Claire would be there. And she planned to make it a night that neither of them would ever forget.

"Do you want me to hang these up or something?" Lucas asked. In his hands were two framed black-and-white photographs.

"Um, I don't know." Kate looked up from her overstuffed trunk. She ran a hand through her long red hair. "I could be gone in a week, and I'd hate to leave nails stuck in the walls for no reason."

"Right," Lucas agreed, putting the photographs

down on top of the dresser he'd moved up from the basement. Now that most of the heavy lifting was done, Lucas began to edge toward the door. The tiny room was cramped enough without him taking up space.

"Well, I guess I'll get out of your way and let you unpack," he said.

"You don't have to go on my account," Kate said. "I kind of like the company."

So far Kate wasn't exactly what Lucas had expected. Aside from being dressed all in black, she didn't seem to be the snobby artist type he'd anticipated.

Lucas wasn't really the best person at making small talk, but he figured that leaving right then might seem rude. And his mother had already given the two of them a whole speech about how she couldn't wait for them to get to know each other. Mrs. Cabral didn't ask much from her only son, or from anyone, really. Lucas figured he could at least try to make an effort.

He picked up the photos from the top of the dresser and took a closer look at them. One was of a fence and sand, but on further inspection, Lucas realized that it wasn't really a fence, only its shadow. The other was of a baby on a playground trying to touch its shadow. Each had Kate's signature in the bottom corner.

"These are really good," Lucas said.

"Thanks," Kate replied. "Those are two of my favorites. They were part of a series I did studying shadows. It really helped me appreciate black-and-white film. You can see the subtleties of shading much better than with color."

So she was an artist type after all. But Lucas had to

cut her some slack. He was the one who had brought the topic up.

"Yeah," Lucas said, for lack of anything else to say. *I'm sure she won't think you're an idiot now*, he thought sarcastically. *Not after such a brilliant response*.

They were quiet for a minute as Lucas looked around for another thing to comment on and Kate continued to sort her clothes in her trunk. Suddenly Kate stopped what she was doing and turned to face Lucas straight on.

"Lucas," Kate began, "I want you to know that I've always considered you like a relative. And I know you were kind of rolling your eyes when your mother said it before, but I really hope we can get closer while I'm staying here. I mean, if it weren't for your grandparents, I probably never would have been born."

"Sure," Lucas responded. Whatever. She wanted to be polite. She was staying in his house, after all.

"I mean," Kate continued, "I know you always thought I was, like, a total geek or something. . . ."

"What?" Lucas was thoroughly surprised. "I never thought you were a geek. You were the one who thought I was an idiot from some hick town."

"No, I didn't," Kate exclaimed. "I always thought you were so cool because you had a dirt bike and got to go fishing all the time with your dad."

"And I always thought that you were so adult because you drank coffee."

"Well, I do have a machine," she said, pointing to the mini Mr. Coffee on her bed.

"I already noticed that," Lucas said with a grin.

They both laughed.

"I have to tell you," Kate said, "I did feel a little

weird about coming to stay here. But now I'm kind of glad.''

"Yeah," Lucas said. "I have a good feeling about this. Who knows? We could end up good friends and make my mother's year."

"My mother's, too," Kate said.

She crossed the room and gave Lucas a hug.

Zoey felt her stomach clamor unhappily as the ferry docked on the island. Instead of going to the mall, she and Aisha had gone for hot chocolate and french fries in Portsmouth. Now Zoey's intestines were getting their revenge on her for all the grease and sugar. What had they been thinking when they'd ordered that second serving of fries?

Zoey turned toward home. Aisha had opted to do some work at the library and take the 7:40 back. Even though it had cost her a trip to the Gap, Zoey was happy for Aisha about the scholarship. It would probably turn her friend into even more of a study geek for the next few weeks, but it was good that Aisha had something to take her mind off Christopher. And Aisha would now have a distraction as Valentine's Day approached. Zoey was selfishly grateful for that, because there was nothing like a cynical, depressed friend to suck the spirit right out of the holiday. In fact, for years Zoey had had to put up with Nina's theorizing about a major conspiracy involving the flower, candy, and greeting card industries.

But this year would be special for Zoey. After all, it was her first Valentine's Day with Lucas. And after the abrupt way Lucas had left her room the night before, she wanted to make sure that he forgave her for Aaron Mendel once and for all.

Besides, Lucas really did love her. And she really

did love him, too. That was reason enough for a special Valentine's Day.

With all of Aisha's excitement, Zoey had almost forgotten Lucas's news. She looked at her watch. 5:30. Lucas's new houseguest had probably arrived. She turned onto South Street. Her curiosity piqued, Zoey decided to drop her stuff off at home and then go to Lucas's to get her first glimpse of Kate Levin.

As it turned out, she didn't have to wait that long. As she headed to her own front door, Zoey glanced up at the Cabrals' house. She squinted to make sure that the fading sun hadn't made her see things. But there were no two ways about it.

In the upstairs window, Zoey could see Lucas hugging a redhead. And even from this distance, Zoey could tell she was a very pretty redhead.

Eight

Jake could feel his eyes losing focus. He'd been sitting at his desk for what seemed like years, making some headway on his *Macbeth* paper. But for the past five minutes he had been unable to write a word.

He glanced over at the clock on his nightstand. 10:12. It was late, but not that late. Jake knew he was too fried to work, but he was still too keyed up to sleep.

Maybe he could exhaust himself enough to be ready for bed. He needed a good night's sleep, even if the next day was Friday. Jake dropped to the floor and did fifty push-ups.

If this had been a few months ago, he knew where he would be: heading for the liquor closet. But not anymore. Right now he had no desire to drink. Jake was sure that this time he would really stay clean.

He surveyed his room, looking for a better way to blow off steam. His gaze came to rest on Lara's painting, which he had propped up on his dresser. He was still deeply touched by the effort that Lara had put into it. It made Jake feel special in a way he hadn't felt since he was with Zoey, in a way he hadn't thought he'd feel again ever since she'd dumped him for Lucas.

It also said a lot about the way Lara saw Jake. In

the painting, he was smiling and gentle. He looked like a person you would count on for support and understanding. Which was strange, because in the months before it was painted, Jake had felt anything but dependable. He had been well on his way to flushing his life down the toilet, exactly as his brother, Wade, had done a few years before.

Still, Lara trusted him. It made Jake feel good to know that someone believed in him and needed him.

Jake checked the clock again. 10:21. It wasn't too late to pay Lara a visit. He didn't have to know exactly how long the two of them would last to know that he liked being with her.

Opening his sliding glass door and heading out into the cold night, Jake smiled to himself. There were certain advantages to seeing a girl with her own apartment, and nighttime visits had to be at the top of the list.

As Jake climbed the steps of the old Victorian mansion-turned-apartment-house, he could almost feel the beat of the house music blasting from Lara's studio apartment.

Well, at least she's awake, Jake thought. He hoped she wasn't in the middle of painting. The door was slightly ajar, and as Jake knocked, it swung fully open.

"Hey, Lar—" he started, then stopped short. Lara was dressed in a tight pink T-shirt and tiny bikini underpants. She was dancing languidly on her unmade bed. It was a scene Jake was all too familiar with. Even before he saw the empty bottle of Wild Turkey rolling on the floor by the bed, Jake knew Lara was wasted.

"Jakie!" she exclaimed, jumping off the bed and running over to hug him. "You're here! I'm so happy to see you!" She flung her arms around his neck.

The alcohol on her breath made Jake want to retch.

He removed her arms from his neck, trying to disengage himself from her flailing embrace.

"What the hell are you doing, Lara?"

"Oh, Jakie, I jus' wanna add some spice to my life," she said. Jake couldn't tell if she was trying to sway to the beat of the music or just unable to stand still.

"I thought you'd had enough of this kind of spice," he said. He peered into her bloodshot blue eyes, trying to guess if she was upset about anything in particular.

"Oh, Jakie." Lara rubbed his face with her ice-cold fingers. "Sweet, kind Jakie. You don't even know." She shook her head in sadness. "You don't even know."

While Lara babbled softly, Jake gently guided her to the edge of the bed, and they both sat down.

"What don't I even know?" he asked, holding her hand. Had one of the Passmores said something to alienate her? He knew they were going through a hard time because of Benjamin, but Jake had thought they understood how fragile Lara was.

"You don't even know," she said, her head rocking back and forth, "how incredibly *boring* everyone on this stupid island is! Daddy-pie and his little Zoey, Lucas and his little Zoey, you . . ."

In a heartbeat Jake felt his sympathy shift to anger. It was bad enough that Lara had broken her promise to stay clean. It was bad enough that by getting wasted she had hurt so many people—herself, the Passmores, Jake. But the way she blamed everyone else for her mistakes made Jake want to scream in frustration. Couldn't she see that he was only trying to help her?

Lara had told him a thousand times how much she appreciated everything he'd done for her. But Jake now realized it had all been lip service—lip service intended to ensure that she got what she wanted, which was Jake's compassion. And it had worked. Even now, finding her drunk alone in her room, Jake had waited patiently for an explanation. Well, there was only one explanation for her behavior, an explanation that Jake had known all along: Lara was just bad news.

"I'm getting out of here, Lara," he said, trying to keep his anger in check as he rose to leave.

"Wait, Jakie, don't leave," she said, trying unsuccessfully to rise from the bed. "At least not before you get what you came for."

She flung off the pink T-shirt, exposing herself to him, then grabbed his thigh and tried to pull him onto the bed beside her. It was the first time that Jake could remember actually being repulsed by the sight of bare breasts.

"This is the last straw," he said, pulling away from her and heading for the door. "And don't bother painting me another picture or telling me how much you've changed. I'm not buying it anymore. It's over, Lara. You can drink yourself to death for all I care. You're on your own."

As he slammed the door in disgust, Jake thought of his own words to Aisha on the ferry that morning. *Sometimes you just have to make a clean break.*

Zoey was so deep into her reading that she jumped when she heard the knock on her door. Who would have ever thought that an article on Brad Pitt could be so absorbing? His last movie had sucked.

"Come in," she called, leaning back in her chair to see the door.

"Hi," Lucas said as he entered her room. "I'm glad I got here before you went to bed."

"Are you?" Zoey asked nonchalantly.

"Well, maybe not," he said, planting a kiss on her neck suggestively.

Return of the hormones, Zoey thought as she rose from her seat, escaping Lucas's embrace. In her opinion, Lucas had had enough cuddling that night with his new housemate.

"How's Kate?" she asked, trying to keep her tone even as she went to sit on her bed.

"Actually, she's not what I expected." Lucas took off his coat.

"Really?" Zoey asked. "I thought you barely remembered Kate."

"I did. But I always thought she didn't like me or something."

"And today she did something to change that impression?" Zoey asked, already knowing the answer but wondering how Lucas would explain the embrace that she had witnessed. If he chose to mention it at all.

"Yeah. Definitely. It's actually kind of funny," he said, sitting down beside her on the bed. "She thought that *I* was the one who didn't like *her*!"

"Imagine that," Zoey mumbled.

"Yeah. But I think it's gonna be kind of nice having her around."

"And why is that?" As if she didn't already know.

"Because I think she's really cool," Lucas began.

Anyone looking into your window could've seen that.

"I mean, her photographs are, like, really amazing," he continued. "And she's really smart, but not in a way that's at all conceited."

"Wow," Zoey said with no enthusiasm, "sounds like Kate made quite an impression on you."

"She really did." Lucas nodded as he answered. "I

69

don't know, it's weird. We're not really family, but there's, like, this bond there—"

I'll bet there is, Zoey thought meanly.

"I mean, Kate and I were talking about the war and our grandparents and everything, and it's pretty amazing when you think about what their lives must have been like, hiding from the Nazis. I always thought it was a really brave thing for my grandparents to have done, but I never really thought about what it must have been like to live in constant fear. If the Nazis had found out my grandparents were hiding Jews, they would have killed all of them—Kate's grandparents, my grandparents, both of our mothers. It's pretty incredible when you think about it."

For a moment Zoey forgot about what she'd seen that evening. "It is pretty amazing. When you think about things like that, it makes you realize that what you consider huge problems are actually so insignificant."

Lucas nodded. "That's just what we were saying."

"We?"

"Yeah, me and Kate."

Suddenly the memory of the hug she'd witnessed hit Zoey like a ton of bricks. She felt herself stiffen.

"I mean, she was saying how grateful she is to our family, you know?" Lucas went on. "She said that without my grandparents, she probably wouldn't be alive. I had never really thought of it like that before."

"I'll bet she's grateful," Zoey said. *Very grateful.* "And just how does she intend to show you her gratitude?"

Lucas furrowed his brow in confusion. "What do you mean? She just wants to get to know us a little better, I guess."

The pointedness of her remark had obviously been

lost on Lucas. It was pretty clear to Zoey by now that he felt no guilt at all. *Lucas is totally oblivious and totally innocent*, Zoey realized. She had completely overreacted.

"So what happened to you tonight?" he asked. "I thought you were going to stop by and meet Kate."

"I was. It's just that I didn't get back until later than I thought, and I wanted to come home and check on Benjamin and everything. By the time we finished dinner, I figured I should give you some time to get better acquainted with Kate." Zoey couldn't tell Lucas the real reason why she hadn't come by. He would think she was ridiculous, and he would be right.

Why had she been so quick to doubt him? She should have learned her lesson with the Lara incident. True, Zoey had walked in on Lara and Lucas in what could have been a compromising position. But even if she still had doubts about her half sister's motives for being in her boyfriend's room, Zoey knew that Lucas hadn't been at all unfaithful to her. Yet at the time she had been so quick to think the worst of him. She had needed Aisha and Christopher to bring her back to her senses and give Lucas the benefit of the doubt. He deserved that from her now.

"Well, I missed you," Lucas said, leaning in to give Zoey one of his intense, amazing kisses.

"Me too," she responded, coming up for air.

As she allowed herself to melt into Lucas's embrace, Zoey vowed never to assume the worst about Lucas again.

Nine

The sound of his alarm hit Benjamin like a sledgehammer. He rolled over and fumbled for the snooze button and the ten-minute reprieve it offered. What was it? Friday? It felt more like a Monday. Then again, there had been no day in Benjamin's recent memory that hadn't felt like a Monday. For the past month Benjamin had been desperately trying to hide under the covers and make the days disappear.

That morning he was once again tempted to do just that.

But he had missed Thursday, not to mention countless other days since Christmas break, and Benjamin knew that soon his absences would catch up with him. His parents had already given him a speech about how they trusted him to make his own decisions. They were trying to give him space, but Benjamin could sense their concern.

Even more troublesome than his parents were his teachers. They all knew what had happened and had all been very understanding (in other words, full of pity). But their sympathy could get him only so far. If Benjamin wasn't careful, he could jeopardize his chances of graduating in the spring.

Again the alarm sounded. Again Benjamin rolled

over and hit the snooze button to squelch its blare.

On the other hand, why bother?

What difference could it possibly make if he graduated that year or not? He certainly hadn't put much effort into the college application process. Even if he got in somewhere, Benjamin doubted he'd actually go. He'd have to acclimate himself to a totally new set of surroundings, which would be no easy feat. He'd have to learn how many steps there were between his dorm room and every classroom, from his classrooms to the dining hall, from the dining hall to the library—trying not to look like a helpless idiot in the process.

A knock on his door interrupted Benjamin's bleak train of thought. Zoey was coming to check up on him, an occurrence that was fast becoming a part of his sister's morning routine.

"Come in, Zo. I'm up," he called.

"Good morning," she said with forced cheerfulness. "I just wanted to see—"

"If I was awake? Well, I am, Zoey."

"Good. So does that mean you're getting out of bed?"

Benjamin sighed audibly. He knew that Zoey was only trying to help, but her nagging was beginning to tear at his already jagged nerves. She was worse than his parents.

"Come on, Benjamin," Zoey cajoled. "You're practically throwing off the weight balance on the ferry."

"Well, it manages to transport the rest of you without my help."

"Yeah, but everyone misses you."

"They miss me, huh?" *Pity me is more like it.*

"Of course they do. And it's not just everyone on the island. People keep coming up to me in the halls and asking how you are. Everyone cares, Benjamin. Nobody wants to see you do this to yourself.''

He was sure that other Weymouth High students came up to Zoey all the time. They were the same people whose pitying comments Benjamin would have to pretend not to hear all day if he went to school:

Isn't it sad what happened to Benjamin Passmore? Did you know that he had an operation to restore his sight and it didn't work?

Poor guy. Can you imagine having to go through something like that?

I don't know what I would do if it were me.

Zoey was still trying to convince him to get out of bed. ''I'll make pancakes for breakfast.''

Before he could answer, his alarm buzzed again. Benjamin reached over and this time turned it off entirely.

''Zoey, I really appreciate what you're trying to do, but I don't think I'm up to school today.''

''Fine,'' she said. The disappointment in her voice was obvious. ''I just don't think it's a good idea for you to sit in the house all day by yourself. It's not going to make you feel any better.''

''You're right, Zoey,'' Benjamin replied, straining to keep the anger out of his tone. ''It's not going to make me feel better. But it's sure as hell not going to make me feel worse.''

''Benjamin—''

''You'd better get a move on, Zoey,'' he said, trying his best to show her that the case was closed.

He heard Zoey's sigh, followed by a creaking sound that told Benjamin the door was closing.

Benjamin rolled over and went back to sleep.

* * *

Aisha paid the cashier and turned the corner to look for the rest of her friends. She craned her neck to try to find the table the rest of the girls had chosen that day, but so far she'd had no luck making them out through the sea of faces in the lunchroom.

Serves me right for coming this late, she thought. But she hadn't had much choice. The battery in her calculator had run out in the middle of calculus, and Aisha had had to go to the school store to replace it before physics. Now that she was in the running for the Westinghouse scholarship, Aisha couldn't afford to come to class unprepared.

Finally she spotted Claire, Nina, and Zoey sitting at a table near the window. Aisha made her way toward them, glancing at the clock and realizing that she had only fifteen minutes left to eat her fish sticks and creamed corn.

"Hi, guys," she said, taking the seat next to Claire. "Sorry I'm late."

"You didn't miss much," Nina grumbled as she sucked on her straw. "Just an analysis of what passes for cream in creamed corn."

"I think I'll pass on that, thanks," Aisha said, cutting off that line of conversation. However disgusting the creamed corn might be, Aisha was famished. She didn't want to diminish her chances of being able to keep the food down.

"Good call, Eesh," Claire said. "By the way, congratulations on the Westinghouse thing."

"Thanks, but I still have a couple of months to study my butt off if I'm gonna actually win the scholarship."

"Sounds fun," Nina said dryly.

"Yeah, well, at least it's something to keep my mind off other things." Aisha sighed. "Like how I completely ruined the best relationship of my life."

"Better to have ruined the relationship than your entire life, which is exactly what you would have done if you'd accepted Christopher's proposal," Claire reasoned.

Aisha nodded as she spooned creamed corn into her mouth. Claire was right. Marrying Christopher at this stage of her life would have been a mistake. She just wished it hadn't cost her Christopher.

"Anyway," Zoey added, "I'm not convinced that you and Christopher are really over. I still think you should write to him."

"I don't know. I wish I could just tell him how I feel, but it's still too complicated."

"Kind of sucks, doesn't it?" Nina mumbled softly.

Aisha looked across the table at her friend. Nina was staring down at her plate and picking at the remnants of her lunch absently. She looked so sad. Aisha felt bad. Here she was complaining about her problems with Christopher again while Nina was obviously going through something just as painful with Benjamin.

"So, Zoey," Aisha said in order to change the subject, "you never told me about Lucas's new houseguest."

"She's a photography student," Zoey said nonchalantly. "Her name's Kate Levin. She goes to the New England Art Institute, and there was some kind of screwup with her housing. Mrs. Cabral and her mother were best friends when they were little girls in Holland, so she offered to let Kate stay with them. Actually, it's a little more intense then that. Lucas's grandparents hid Kate's mother and her family in their basement during the war."

"Like, from the Nazis?" Nina's eyes were wide.

"Exactly," Zoey replied.

"Wow," Nina began, "that's like something out of a TV movie. It's like *The Diary of Anne Frank* without a diary!"

"Or Anne Frank," Aisha pointed out as she chewed.

"I never even knew that Lucas's grandparents did that," Nina commented.

"Neither did I," Zoey said. "I don't think Lucas himself really thought about it until Kate showed up."

"You still haven't answered my question. What is she like?" Aisha dipped her forkful of fish into some ketchup. Dousing the stuff in condiments always made cafeteria food somewhat easier to swallow.

"I don't know," Zoey answered with a shrug. "I haven't met her yet."

"Why not?" Nina asked. "It's not every day that someone new comes to Chatham Island. At least not until tourist season."

"I, um, just got distracted by other things," Zoey said. "It got too late."

That was strange. Aisha distinctly remembered Zoey saying she was going to Lucas's when the two of them had left the diner the previous afternoon. Maybe something had come up with Benjamin. Whatever it was, Zoey obviously didn't want to discuss it.

Just then Aisha felt a tap on her shoulder. She turned around to see David Barnes standing behind her.

"David," she said, confused. "What's up?"

She and David had a lot of classes together but rarely conversed outside of the classroom. He probably wanted to borrow her physics notes or something.

"I just wanted to congratulate you on being a Westinghouse finalist," he said with a smile.

"Oh, thanks," she replied with slight surprise. "How did you know about that?"

"Then you haven't heard?" he said, his blue eyes twinkling from behind his tortoiseshell glasses. "It's you and me."

Now Aisha was really baffled. "I thought they didn't announce the winner for another month."

He chuckled. "They don't. Until then, it's *either* me or you. We're the only ones in the running."

"Oh," she said. "Then congratulations to you, too."

"Thank you," he said with a smirk. "You know, you should probably enjoy being a finalist while you can, because I'm going to win the scholarship."

"Is that so?" Aisha asked.

"Yes, it is," David said, turning on his heel and walking away.

Aisha could feel her blood beginning to boil. "Of all the smug, conceited—"

"Aisha," Claire said, "don't tell me that you're falling for that act."

"What act?"

Claire sighed. "That's the oldest trick in the book," she said matter-of-factly. "He's just trying to psych out the competition. Frankly, the way he went about it shows a real lack of imagination."

"Well, I'm not giving up on my chance at this scholarship just because David Barnes thinks he's better than me."

"Claire's right, Eesh," Zoey said. "You shouldn't let him get to you."

"Don't worry," Aisha responded as she cast a glance back at David, who was strutting cockily toward his table. "I have no intention of letting him intimidate me."

Ten

Nina tried to readjust the position of her foot by taking it out from between two of the couch cushions, but it was no use. The pins-and-needles feeling was already upon her. Her foot was totally asleep.

She lifted her leg from the Passmores' couch, shaking it to try to get the circulation flowing again.

"What are you doing?" Benjamin asked from the other end of the sofa.

Nina was almost pleased. It was only the tenth thing he'd said to her all night, but at least it showed that her boyfriend was, in fact, aware of her presence. She was beginning to doubt whether or not he remembered that she'd been sitting there with him and watching TV all night.

"Shaking my foot. It's either asleep or having an allergic reaction to Barbara Walters."

"Oh," he said.

Nina tried to decide whether that exchange qualified as a conversation and realized that this was becoming truly pathetic. It was Friday night, and she and Benjamin were watching a report on radon gas in some elementary school in Cleveland. She had been trying all night to take Mrs. Passmore's advice and give Benjamin some space, but there was no way that watching this show was going to help Benjamin out of his funk.

"You know, Benjamin," Nina began, "I think I've had enough Friday night TV to last me through at least the next three months. I don't think I can take any more."

"I agree," he said, fumbling under his blanket for the remote control. Benjamin fished it out and turned off the television, leaving them to sit in the quiet darkness of the family room.

Nina listened for a moment to the sound of the refrigerator in the nearby kitchen. She waited for Benjamin to initiate a new activity.

Just give him space. She repeated the words in her head for what seemed like the fiftieth time that night.

After a few minutes of sitting in silence, Nina could take it no longer. "So, what should we do now?" she asked.

"Whatever." Benjamin answered with the apathy that was fast becoming his tone of choice.

"If you want, I could read to you," she offered.

"I don't think I'd pay very good attention," he replied.

So much for that, Nina thought. She opened her mouth to offer another idea, but Mrs. Passmore's words came back to haunt her. *Just give him space.* It was becoming a mantra.

Nina eased back against the sofa cushions and tried to relax. Maybe she could just close her eyes and take a little nap. That would kill some time. She wondered if Benjamin would notice that she was asleep at the other end of the couch. Only if she snored, she figured.

A minute later Nina felt Benjamin's leg stir underneath the blanket. He had shifted slightly, and their legs were now touching. Nina felt a tingle run up her thigh. Benjamin had initiated bodily contact!

She reached under the blanket and started to rub his calf. "Do you want to go up to your room?" She kept her voice soft, although nobody was home yet.

"What?" Benjamin asked.

"Do you want to go up to your room? Zoey could be back soon, and that way we could definitely, you know, have some privacy."

He pulled his leg away from her. Although it was too dark for her to tell for sure, Nina thought Benjamin had sat up on the couch.

"Nina, that's not going to happen tonight," he said shortly.

"But I thought—"

"Well, then, you obviously thought wrong."

Nina couldn't just sit silently anymore. All of this tiptoeing around was making her crazy. She had to tell Benjamin what she was thinking.

"I can't stand to see you like this, Benjamin. It's just not like you to be so—"

"Depressed?"

"That, too. But what I meant was wallowing in self-pity."

He laughed. "Why shouldn't I? There's certainly enough pity around here for me to wallow in. You pity me, my parents pity me, Zoey pities me. You name 'em, they pity me. If you can't beat 'em, join 'em."

"We do not pity you, Benjamin. We miss you. You just haven't been yourself—"

"No, I've been myself. I just haven't been the great blind wonder. I don't have the energy for it anymore."

"That's because you're wasting all of your energy on being depressed."

"Why shouldn't I be depressed?" he shouted into the darkness. "I can't see, Nina. I'll never see! You can't know what it's like. Nobody can!"

Nina stared into the blackness of the room, her heart aching because she knew he was right. Even sitting there in the dark, she could still see the VCR clock. Even if she walked around with a blindfold on, bits of light would probably get through. And her sight would always be a flick of the light switch away. Benjamin's never would be.

Hearing him sob softly, Nina rose from her end of the couch and felt her way to his side. She had never heard Benjamin cry before. Maybe now he was finally letting Nina in, sharing his pain with her. It was the only thing she'd wanted these past weeks. Nina wrapped her arms around Benjamin, trying desperately to comfort him.

His response hit her like a stab in the chest. "Nina," he said, freeing himself from her embrace, "I think you should leave."

Zoey felt the sting of cold winter air as she headed out of Passmores' and onto Dock Street. Normally Lara was supposed to waitress on Friday nights, but she'd called in sick with what she said was the stomach flu.

Zoey had her suspicions about the true nature of Lara's "illness." She knew that since being kicked out of the Passmore home, Lara had supposedly been clean and sober. But it couldn't be that easy to quit drinking.

Since she couldn't do anything about it, Zoey resolved not to think about Lara McAvoy any more than she had to. And she didn't have to now, since she was on her way to Lucas's house to watch a video. And to finally meet Kate Levin.

Zoey shivered as she headed up South Street. The temperature must have dropped at least fifteen degrees since she'd left her house that evening. It was only

February, but it seemed as if it had been winter forever. Zoey quickened her pace.

She approached his front door and turned the knob, trying not to make too much noise as she entered the Cabrals' house. Mr. Cabral worked every day except Sunday, and Zoey knew that he and Mrs. Cabral were already asleep.

As she tiptoed through the small foyer and up the stairs, Zoey couldn't shake the feeling of déjà vu. It had been only about a month since she'd last entered this house the same way, only to find Lara sprawled out on her boyfriend's bed. Although Lara had denied it, Zoey knew that her half sister had been there for one reason only—to hook up with Lucas. Was it any wonder that Zoey couldn't trust that girl?

She knocked softly on Lucas's door.

A girl's voice answered. "Come in."

Zoey opened the door and gasped. Lucas was kneeling on the floor in front of a beautiful redhead. His head was bent, almost as if he were praying, and his long blond hair fell over his eyes. The redhead sat perched on the edge of a large black trunk. She gazed down at Lucas expectantly. Zoey noted that they weren't even an inch apart and Lucas's head was practically in her lap.

"Lucas!" she said, her voice sounding high-pitched and breathless in her own ears.

"Hey, Zoey." Lucas didn't look up. "I wasn't expecting you so early."

"I guess not." She noticed that his eyes were fixed on a point midway down the redhead's black velvet leggings.

"Hi," the redhead said. "I'm Kate. You must be the famous Zoey. I've heard a lot about you." Kate held out her hand, but she didn't rise from her seat on the trunk.

"Really?" A chain of confused, disconnected thoughts and questions were flying through Zoey's head. *Is this some sort of art school thing? Some perverse love/sculpture activity? Only it's not a sculpture. It's more of a pose. Or something.*

"I almost forgot that you guys hadn't met yet." Lucas finally rose to his feet. "I guess we got it," he said to Kate.

"What did you get?" Zoey asked quickly.

"The trunk to close," Kate said, rising as well. "The latch on this thing is so old, it takes two people to close it. Lucas was nice enough to help me out."

"How was subbing for Lara?" Lucas asked as he put his arm around Zoey's shoulder.

Zoey hurriedly pulled her bizarre thoughts back into gear. "The usual," she said.

He was acting so normal. Obviously nothing weird was going on at all. Despite her vow of the night before, Zoey had jumped to conclusions yet again. She had allowed herself to imagine the worst of Lucas.

"I think it's so cool that your family has a restaurant, Zoey. It must be really nice to have everyone working together." Kate ran a hand through her thick, fiery mane of hair. Shiny and wavy, it was like the hair in shampoo commercials, and the total opposite of Zoey's shapeless dark blond mop.

"Yeah. Well, the restaurant can be a pain sometimes," Zoey said. "Like when you have to give up your Friday nights to cover someone else's shift."

"I rented a movie, so we can go watch it now if you feel like it," Lucas offered.

"Great," Zoey said, eager to clear her head and get on with her evening. Lucas's houseguest would be perfectly fine left to her own devices. "What did you get?"

"*Annie Hall*. Kate says it's, like, the best movie ever. I didn't think you'd seen it."

So now Kate was choosing their movie. It figured, Zoey thought. After all, Lucas was obviously quite impressed with her. "No, I haven't seen it." Zoey turned to take off her coat and put it on the desk chair. Out of the corner of her eye, she saw Kate begin to drag her trunk out of the room and into the hallway.

"Wait, Kate," Lucas said. "You're watching with us, right?"

"I don't know." Kate glanced in Zoey's direction. "I wouldn't want to intrude." Her voice dripped with sincere politeness.

Of course you wouldn't, Kate.

"No way," Lucas replied. "You can't make me get a movie and then not sit and watch it with us. You wouldn't be intruding. Right, Zoey?"

Zoey had no choice. If she said she didn't want Kate to watch it with them, then she'd look like a bitch. "Of course not."

"Great," Kate said, her brown eyes brightening. "I'll just put the trunk back in my room and meet you guys down there."

"Great," Lucas said, beaming.

"Great," Zoey mumbled inaudibly. She wondered if she would ever have Lucas to herself again.

A Weekend

SATURDAY

9 A.M.

Aisha stops hitting her snooze button and gets out of bed. She has a long day of studying ahead of her.

12 NOON

Zoey wakes up to find Lucas in her room.

"I thought we could do what we didn't get to do last night," he says.

He joins her under the covers, but after five minutes of intense kissing, he suggests that they get up and do something. With Kate.

3 P.M.

Nina and Claire return from lunch in Weymouth with their father and Sarah Mendel.

Nina thinks she may have finally convinced them not to make her wear one of those frilly bridesmaid's dresses to their wedding.

Claire reminds her that whatever she wears will still have to be lilac, Sarah's favorite color.

5 P.M.

Zoey and Lucas return from giving Kate a tour of the island.

If Kate had taken one more picture or made one more comment about how lucky they were to have grown up surrounded by such natural beauty, Zoey would have thrown up.

If Lucas had said "Isn't she great?" one more time, Zoey would have punched him.

7 P.M.

Benjamin decides to take his first shower in five days. His smell is finally beginning to get to him.

When he gets out, Zoey tells him that Nina called. He decides not to call her back.

9 P.M.

Jake attends an AA meeting. He speaks about ending things with Lara. After the meeting, two people stop him and tell him he did the right thing. One of those people is Louise Kronenberger.

11 P.M.

Aisha returns to the island on the last ferry. She falls asleep ten minutes after returning home.

12 MIDNIGHT

Zoey and Lucas fall asleep watching *Saturday Night Live*. Finally Kate found something to do with her time other than hang out with Lucas.

SUNDAY
8:30 A.M.

Aisha wakes up to discover that she's slept in her clothes. She rises, showers, and heads back to the library in Weymouth.

11 A.M.

Jake returns home from church to finish his *Macbeth* paper.

2 P.M.

Nina debates stopping by the Passmores' house. She decides not to, since Benjamin hasn't even called her back yet. She's giving him space.

3 P.M.

All this space is making Nina crazy. She has to do something. In a burst of nervous energy, she heads to the drugstore and buys red hair dye.

4 P.M.

Claire talks to Aaron on the phone. He's glad she can come to the Valentine's Day party in Portland. She tells him she has a surprise in store for him that night.

7 P.M.

Zoey and Lucas return from a day in Portside with Kate. Zoey noticed that Kate touched Lucas's sleeve a total of six times. *Bitch*.

8 P.M.

Aisha returns from the library. Her father is proud of her determination. Her mother warns her not to go overboard. Her brother, Kalif, is happy to have had her out of the house all weekend.

9 P.M.

Nina stares at herself in the mirror. The red hair doesn't really match her skin coloring. She figures it doesn't matter. Benjamin won't know the difference, and he's the only one whose opinion she really cares about.

9:30 P.M.

Benjamin calls Nina and apologizes. He's just been in a funk. She knows, and is happy he called.

10 P.M.

Lucas and Kate have hot cocoa before he goes to bed. Kate doesn't have classes on Mondays until eleven. This makes Lucas more excited about college than before.

Lucas tells Kate that he's glad there's someone else

in the house who stays up past nine o'clock. He's also glad she and Zoey get along so well.

11 P.M.

Jake finally finishes his *Macbeth* paper.

Claire

Webster's lists a total of nine definitions for the word <u>love.</u> The first is "a strong affection for another arising out of kinship or personal ties." Aaron and I certainly have both.

We understand and appreciate each other because we're so alike. And our feeling of kinship will be solidified into legal fact when our parents get married. Of course, knowing that he's going to be my stepbrother makes some ~~people~~ my sister, for one ~~uncomfortable~~ with the nature of our relationship. I just think it makes things more convenient. Still, I've decided not to let my father in on the true nature of my feelings for Aaron. He's in his own little dream world with Sarah. Why complicate things unnecessarily?

The second definition Webster's offers is "attraction based on sexual desire: affection and tenderness felt by lovers." That also applies, at least the first part. As of yet, Aaron and I are technically not lovers. In fact, I have technically never had a lover, though I like to come off as vastly experienced.

Of course I've had boyfriends—but I've never taken things to that level. It's been a close call on a couple of occasions, but I guess that deep down inside I'm sort of old-fashioned about that. Not that I believe a person should necessarily wait until they're married before they have sex, but I do feel that having sex, especially for the first time, should be with someone you really care about and who you know really cares about you. I never had that, so I never had sex.

When Lucas and I were a couple, I was only fourteen years old. The idea of sex crossed my mind, and I'm sure it crossed his, but we were too young for it to really become an issue. But later, when we fooled around in my father's car, I was tempted. Even if he's not exactly Einstein, Lucas can be a very sexy guy on a purely physical level. In fact, that's what stopped me. The whole thing was purely physical. Well, not purely physical —half was physical desire and half was the desire for revenge on Jake and Zoey. Actually, the latter was more than half of my motivation. Anyway, it would have been a serious mistake.

And with Jake, well, maybe if we'd been together longer, something could have happened. But as it turned out, I spent a lot more energy on getting him than I did on being with him. Or fooling around with him.

That leaves Benjamin. We were going out for a long time, so that wasn't why we didn't. There were a couple of times when we came pretty close, but one or the other of us would inevitably put a stop to it. I don't think that either one of us wanted to be that intimate. I guess on some level that would have made us more vulnerable to each other, and neither one of us wanted that.

So that's why I'm still a virgin. The simple fact is that the right guy hasn't come along. Until now.

Eleven

"Oh, my God," Claire said, her jaw dropping as her sister entered the kitchen. She tried not to spill coffee all over herself from sheer surprise. Nina's hair was bright red. "What did you do to your hair?"

"Good morning to you, too, Claire," Nina said cheerily.

"I take it Dad has yet to see your new look?"

"If you are referring to the color of my hair, no, he hasn't seen it yet," Nina said, grabbing a bowl and joining Claire at the table. "In fact, up until a minute ago I wasn't sure I liked it. But the expression on your face just now made it all worthwhile."

Claire rolled her eyes. "Well, I'm glad to be of service. I hope it's some comfort to you whenever you look in the mirror and see how ridiculous that hair color is."

"I'm sure it will be," Nina responded with a smile.

At least this cloud has a silver lining, Claire thought. After weeks of being unhappy, Nina was acting like her normal freakish self again. Maybe Claire could finally stop worrying about her now. Nina's tension had been the only thing keeping Claire from feeling all-out blissful about Aaron. Now she could revel in her joy unencumbered.

"Good morn—" Just as Claire had anticipated, Burke Geiger stopped in midphrase when he noticed the change in his younger daughter's hair coloring.

"Hi, Dad," Nina responded with what Claire knew to be deliberate nonchalance.

"Nina, your hair . . ."

"Yeah. Do you like it?" Nina asked, putting on her best eager-to-please face.

"Well, it's very . . . red," her father said finally.

"I know," Nina said, spooning cereal into her mouth. "I thought I'd try out some new looks before the wedding."

Claire could do nothing but admire the sheer brilliance of her sister's strategy. By making her ridiculous foray into the world of Nice 'n Easy into a part of the general wedding mania, Nina had given their father no choice but to swallow his disgust. Claire couldn't have played it better herself.

"Well . . ." Her father fumbled for a comment as he poured his morning coffee. "That's an . . . er . . . interesting idea."

"That's okay, Dad," Nina said as she rose and patted her father on the back. "I'm a little on the fence about it myself. I don't think it'll look good with lilac."

Claire doubted her father had picked up on Nina's parting shot at the color scheme, but she was still impressed with her sister's performance. Quick conversation, quick exit. By the time their father's head stopped spinning, he wouldn't know what he thought of the dye job.

In addition to making Claire proud, Nina's maneuverings had had another unintended benefit. They had left Burke Geiger confused and vulnerable: Now was the perfect time for Claire to move in for the kill.

"So, Dad," Claire began, "you and Sarah must have big plans for Friday."

At the mention of Valentine's Day, his facial expression did a complete 180-degree turn, from bewildered to bemused. He really had become a sap.

"Actually, I have a bit of a surprise in store for her." Her father was almost beaming.

"Your secret's safe with me, Dad."

"Well, okay. But not the slightest hint. And not a word to your sister."

"Scout's honor," Claire said.

"Sarah doesn't know it yet, but we're spending the weekend in New York City. She thinks we're having dinner in Burlington, but we're really just going there to hop on the plane!"

"Wow, Dad," Claire replied, "that's definitely romantic."

"I bet you didn't think your old dad had it in him."

"Of course I did," Claire said, playing along. This was not the answer she had hoped for. If her father and the merry gnome were going to Burlington, they were probably taking his car. Which meant that Claire couldn't have it herself. Which meant she'd have to find another way to get to Portland. And to Aaron.

"So what are your plans, honey? Do you have anyone, uh, special to spend Valentine's Day with this year?"

Claire bit the inside of her cheek to keep from laughing. It still amazed her that her father and Sarah were so oblivious to what was going on between their children. Before he left, Aaron had hinted to his mother about their romantic involvement. But then he'd gone off to boarding school and left Claire to deal with the parental units. She had decided that the less said on the subject the better. What they didn't know wouldn't hurt them.

"It's more like a lot of someones," Claire lied. "There's a big party in Portland that Aaron told me about. He's coming up for it, so I thought I might go."

"Hmmm. How were you planning on getting down there?"

"I don't know. Bus, I guess." Claire took a sip of coffee. "Aaron and his friends could meet me at the bus station and give me a ride to the party."

Burke Geiger furrowed his brow. "I don't know if I want you hanging around the Portland bus station at night alone."

"Dad, I'm a big girl. Besides, how else am I going to get there? You and Sarah are taking the car to Burlington, right?"

"Well, I had thought so. But we could take Sarah's car instead. That way you can just drive down there and eliminate the bus altogether."

"I don't want to put you out, Dad. I can take the bus. It's no big deal."

"No, Claire. I'd really prefer that you drive."

"If that's what you want—"

"That's what I want," he replied firmly. "Come to think of it, I don't want you to drive home late at night. Why don't you just get a hotel room down in Portland? That way you can stay the night and drive home fresh in the morning when it's light out."

"I don't know, Dad," Claire said with pretend concern. "I wouldn't even know where to stay."

"Don't worry about that. The bank has a discounted rate at the Ritz-Carlton. I'll have my secretary make the reservation today. Just put it on my gold card."

"Dad, I really don't think—"

He raised his hand in protest. "I know you're a big

girl, and I know I sound like a worrywart. Just humor me, Claire. I don't have much longer to be an over-protective father.''

"Well, if you insist," she said, rising to put on her coat and head out for the ferry. "Thanks, Dad."

As she kissed her father's cheek Claire sighed in satisfaction. Everything was going just as she'd planned. It was as if Cupid himself were intervening on Claire's behalf. The burden of endless analyzing, planning, and manipulating had been lifted from her shoulders. She had finally met someone who negated the necessity for subterfuge and struggle. She felt strangely light and utterly relaxed. Cupid would ensure that Friday night was every bit as memorable as she dreamed it would be.

"It's not that I don't like it," Zoey said as delicately as possible, "it's just that it's . . . well, it's really red."

"If you're trying to tell me I look like Bozo the Clown, you should just come out and say it, Zoey. I promise I won't be offended," Nina replied.

Zoey and Aisha had been trying to recover from the shock ever since Nina had taken off her hat and revealed her new hair color. Zoey figured it would take the rest of the ferry ride to do so. If nothing else, at least Nina's hair had broken the usual glum Monday morning routine.

"You do not look like Bozo the Clown." Zoey began. "But it definitely looks different."

"Since when have you wanted to dye your hair? And why didn't you call one of us to guide you?" Aisha's tone was one of true bafflement. "What were you thinking?"

Nina shrugged. "I was just feeling a little bored. It's only hair. Besides, I can dye it back if I want."

"That's true," Zoey conceded, happy that her friend was being reasonable. She doubted that Nina would be able to stand the color for more than a week.

"I've got to hand it to you, Nina," Aisha said. "Between those army fatigues and your new hair, you are single-handedly taking up the alienated-teen banner for the rest of us."

"I do what I can," Nina responded, sticking a Lucky Strike in her mouth and sucking.

"Nina, wow, your hair looks—" After chatting with Jake, Lucas had approached the threesome. He casually put his arm around Zoey.

"Red?" Nina completed his dangling sentence.

"Yeah. Red," he said with a nod.

"Don't tell me. You hate it, too," Nina grumbled.

"No. I think red hair is cool," Lucas replied.

I'll bet you do, Zoey thought with displeasure. Spending practically her whole weekend watching Kate Levin gush at Lucas's every word had been bad enough. But listening to more of Lucas's ravings about Kate the Great was getting on Zoey's last nerve.

But as she looked over at Lucas, Zoey softened. Lucas was wearing her favorite sweatshirt—the Dartmouth one that brought out the flecks of green in his hazel eyes. His arm was around her, not Kate. She was Lucas's girlfriend, and no matter how much Kate bonded with him, what Zoey had with Lucas was special. She would never let it go.

Zoey suddenly realized that Nina had not stopped talking since Lucas's comment.

". . . Lucille Ball, who was one of the greatest comedic geniuses ever. Come to think of it, I should have gone red years ago."

"Whatever you say, Nina," Aisha responded, rolling her eyes.

Nina sighed in mock frustration. "You know, I don't need this kind of pessimism," she said, turning on her heel. "There are people on this ferry who are beyond such superficial things as hair color." She headed to the other side of the ferry, where Benjamin sat listening to his Walkman.

"One thing you can say about the girl," Aisha said with a sigh, "is that there's never a dull moment."

"That's true," Zoey agreed.

"Why'd she dye her hair, anyway?" Lucas asked.

Zoey looked over at Nina and her brother. Benjamin had taken off his earphones and was listening as Nina spoke to him.

"She's had a lot on her mind lately," Zoey said. "She probably needed to blow off some steam."

Zoey's meaning was not lost on either Aisha or Lucas. They both nodded understandingly.

"Well," Aisha said brightly, "he is coming back to school. That's a step in the right direction."

"Yeah, Zo," Lucas agreed. "And he came on his own, without anyone asking him to."

"I hope you're right," Zoey said. "I just think that Benjamin is going through more stuff than any of us understands."

She glanced back at the bench. Benjamin and Nina were holding hands. Maybe Lucas and Aisha were right. Maybe Benjamin was taking the first step toward recovery. Zoey hoped so, not just for his sake but for Nina's as well.

Twelve

In what had become her habitual study spot in the library, Aisha sat squinting down at a chapter entitled "Friction." Her stomach grumbled slightly, but she knew it was not yet time for dinner. She'd just checked the clock, and it wasn't even five-thirty. Like it or not, she still had an hour left before she could leave to catch the 6:40 ferry.

Aisha put her elbows on the table and began rubbing her eyes. She'd spent her whole weekend sitting in this very spot, doing this very thing. Her brain was fried. Why not just leave now and start fresh after dinner?

She could kill an hour somewhere else before going home. She could definitely use a change of scenery. But where? It was too cold to just wander around Weymouth aimlessly. Aisha needed a mission.

She looked over at the circulation desk. Hanging prominently was a poster with Martin Luther King Jr.'s picture on it. February Is Black History Month, it read. Aisha stifled a laugh. Her friends back in Boston had always joked that February had been made Black History Month because it was the shortest month of the year.

Next to that poster was one with a huge red heart on it. Its flowery lettering said, Reading Is Romantic—

Celebrate Valentine's Day with a Book. Aisha sighed. This Valentine's Day was going to be truly pathetic. She would indeed be spending it with a book—her physics book. As much as she wanted to, she was convinced she wouldn't hear from Christopher.

But why should that stop her from doing something for him? Valentine's Day was the perfect excuse to let him know she still cared without being too heavy-handed about it. Aisha rose from her seat, knowing exactly what she'd do before catching the ferry. She'd head to the drugstore and buy Christopher a Valentine's Day card.

As she gathered up her books Aisha felt someone's eyes on her. She looked up to find David Barnes meeting her gaze from a table across the room.

"Leaving already?" he mouthed. The corners of his lips turned upward to form his usual cocky grin.

Damn him, Aisha thought. She couldn't go now. It would give David too much satisfaction. Christopher's card could wait.

"You wish," she mouthed back to David.

As she sat back down and reopened her textbook, Aisha felt a second wind coming on. She still had forty-five minutes to get some productive studying done.

Zoey sat at her kitchen table eating cold leftover spaghetti. She knew it would probably ruin her appetite for dinner, but at the moment she didn't care. Having spent the past hour conjugating French verbs in the pluperfect, Zoey felt entitled to a break.

Besides, she needed to do something to keep her mind from wandering back to the subject of Kate. How could Lucas stand her, anyway? All weekend Kate had been gushing about everything, trying to make herself sound so intellectual. It had all sounded pretentious and phony to Zoey, but Lucas had, for some unknown reason, eaten up every word.

She looked out the window toward the setting sun. It was only Monday. She still had four more days of school until the weekend, but only three left to decide what to do for Lucas for Valentine's Day.

For Valentine's Days past, Zoey had been with Jake. They had always done the standard things—he bought her a stuffed animal or some chocolates, and she got him a card. But this year finding the right gift for her boyfriend was no easy task. Zoey was determined to get Lucas something special.

In fact, she had crossed nearly everything off her mental list already. She had gotten him a wallet for Christmas, so anything leather would seem redundant. Initially Zoey had thought of silk boxer shorts. They had seemed the perfect gift—romantic yet masculine. But on second thought, given Lucas's one-track mind, Zoey had decided that buying underwear could perhaps send the wrong signal.

Guys are impossible to shop for, Zoey decided, shaking her head with finality.

Still, she wanted to make this Valentine's Day special. It was the first year she and Lucas were a couple. They had already gone through so much together—more in a few months than she'd gone through with Jake in years. No matter how selfish or moody she'd been, Lucas had always been there for her. Plus, although his kisses were as hot as ever, the word *sex* hadn't once crossed her boyfriend's lips the whole weekend. If he was still upset about her affair with Aaron, the last thing Zoey wanted was to skimp on his Valentine's Day present.

She peered out her kitchen window and up the hill

to Lucas's house. Zoey thought she could make out a figure walking in the Cabrals' kitchen. She ducked down to get a better glimpse, rationalizing that it wasn't really spying. If it was Lucas, she'd wave.

Zoey saw the dark green sweatshirt and lifted her arm, but a second later she dropped her hand. It was Lucas's sweatshirt, all right, but the person wearing it wasn't him. And it was pretty obvious to Zoey that she wasn't wearing anything else, either.

"Well, that wasn't too brutal," Louise said as she walked down the church steps. "I think it helped that there were so few people there. You know, the less the merrier."

Jake nodded in agreement. This had been the lightest AA meeting he'd gone to since starting the program. Only one person had spoken about falling off the wagon that weekend. The rest, like Jake, had spoken about not even being tempted to drink. "There also weren't any first-timers. That always adds to it," Jake put in. "And I don't think the afternoon meetings get as many people as the night ones."

"Yeah. Most people are just getting out of work now," Louise said.

Jake nodded. The sun was just setting. It couldn't have been past six o'clock. The eight o'clock meeting that night would probably draw a bigger crowd.

"I know I say this to you all the time, Jake, but I'm really glad you're going through the program. It's nice to have someone I know at meetings."

"Yeah," he said, "I'm glad you're there, too. And not just because I know you needed it," he said with a laugh. He knew Louise wouldn't be sensitive about her past behavior. Owning up to it was part of the process of staying clean, and Jake was really impressed by how honest Louise had been about her alcohol-induced wanton ways.

"Well, if anyone knows that, it's you," she said with a wry smile. "It's funny. I mean, we shared a real low point when we were both drinking, and now we're sharing the high point of getting straight."

Jake felt his stomach tighten. He knew what Louise meant, though it was a thought that he tried to fight off every time he saw her. But neither one of them had forgotten the night of homecoming. They had both been wasted and had wound up having sex at some party. Jake had been so messed up that he'd had to be told about the incident. Louise was right; it had definitely been a low point.

"We're both different people now than we were this fall," Jake told her. "Lucky for both of us."

Louise nodded. "That's for sure."

They walked a bit more, each involved in their own thoughts.

"I'm not looking forward to Friday," Louise said, breaking the silence. "It's going to be pretty tempting to take a drink."

"Why's that?" Jake asked.

"The whole Valentine's thing. It's just going to remind me of all the mistakes I made with guys. Present company included."

Jake had almost forgotten that Valentine's Day was right around the corner. Not that it mattered, anyway. He hadn't really planned on celebrating the holiday this year. Whatever the nature of his relationship with Lara had been, he didn't think it extended to corny cards and flowers. But now that things were over between them, Jake definitely didn't have Valentine's plans.

"Well, I'll be at the meeting for sure," he said.

"You don't have any other plans?" Louise asked. The look in her eye seemed hopeful.

"Just the usual Friday night for me. I'll save you a seat at the meeting."

"Great," she said. "Maybe we could get dinner afterward. Maybe catch a movie or something."

"Sounds like a plan," he said.

"I know I said this already, Jake, but I'm so happy we're friends. It means a lot to me to be able to start fresh with you."

"It means a lot to me, too," Jake said. He meant it. Being friends with Louise now, with both of them being in AA, made Jake feel less disgusted about the way he'd lost his virginity.

Louise reached over and gave him a hug, which Jake gladly reciprocated. It felt good to be in her arms, surprisingly good. Jake was beginning to feel things for Louise that had nothing to do with AA meetings or making up for the past. This hug was going on for too long. What did it mean? Were he and Louise . . . ?

Jake disengaged himself from the hug. This was the old Jake, just doing things on impulse. He needed to get his head straight before things progressed any further—if they were even going to at all.

Jake opened his mouth to say something but was struck dumb. There, across the street, stood Lara, eyes blazing.

Thirteen

The cold air stung Zoey's face as she raced over to
Lucas's house. She'd barely remembered to grab her
coat when she headed out her front door, determined
to confront Kate and Lucas about what was obviously
going on between them.

Zoey couldn't remember the last time she'd been so
boiling mad. When she'd first caught her mother
having an affair, she had been too stunned to get angry. But not this time. No, this she'd seen coming from
a mile away.

Zoey had known from the moment she first laid eyes
on Kate Levin that the girl was after Lucas. But she'd
even pretended to be friendly to Kate all weekend for
Lucas's sake.

Well, I'm sorry, she thought, *but all of this sister-
he-never-had stuff has gone too far when she's walking around in the sweatshirt he was wearing this
afternoon.*

She pounded on the Cabrals' front door.

A moment later Kate appeared. "Hey, Zoey," she
said with a smile. "Come on in."

Just as Zoey had suspected, Kate was standing before her wearing Lucas's Dartmouth sweatshirt without

any pants, or socks for that matter. Her long red hair was pulled back in a ponytail.

"Nice sweatshirt," Zoey said.

"Oh." Kate looked down at the shirt, which barely covered half of her thigh. "It's not mine."

"I realize that," Zoey said coldly.

"I'm in the middle of doing laundry, so I needed something to wear while my stuff dried." Kate looked confused, and her face was flushed—*with guilt, perhaps*? Zoey thought. "I found this on the bathroom floor and figured Lucas wouldn't mind. I didn't do anything wrong here, did I? This sweatshirt doesn't have some kind of sentimental value to you guys or something, does it?"

As much as she didn't like to, Zoey had to give her credit. Kate didn't drop the innocent act for a second. Now she was acting as if she was concerned about stepping on Zoey's territory. What a laugh! Well, two could play at that game.

"Don't worry about it, Kate," Zoey said dismissively. "Lucas thinks of you as practically a sister." *That should put her in her place.*

"Really?" Kate blushed even deeper. "Did he say that to you?"

"Yeah," Zoey replied dryly. "He says that all the time."

"That's so sweet," Kate said. "I'm sure you know this already, Zoey, but you've got yourself one great guy."

"I did know that already," she responded. "And if you don't mind, I think I'll go see him now." *And give him a piece of my mind.*

"Oh, you can't do that."

I can't do that? Excuse me? Just who did Kate think she was? And what exactly was she trying to hide by keeping Zoey away from Lucas? Zoey felt the rage spring up in her again. They couldn't have been—

"He's out running an errand for his mom," Kate was saying. "He should be back in a few minutes, though."

Lucas was probably in his room half dressed or, even worse, undressed. There was no way Zoey would let Kate get rid of her so easily.

"Then I guess I'll just go up there and leave him a note," Zoey replied, calling Kate's bluff as she headed toward the stairs.

"Okay," Kate said, leaving the foyer.

Kate had reached so calmly that Zoey wondered if she could have been telling the truth. Was Lucas really not there?

There was only one way to find out. Zoey climbed the stairs and saw Lucas's closed door. She steeled herself for what might be behind it as she reached for the knob and opened it.

The room was empty. Lucas was nowhere in sight. Zoey suddenly realized that she'd been incredibly stupid; then she immediately felt a pang of guilt. She had mistrusted Lucas yet again.

She went downstairs and headed for the door, feeling like a huge idiot, an undeserving girlfriend. She had expected to catch Lucas in the middle of cheating on her, just the way he'd caught her in the arms of Aaron Mendel. But, as usual, her instincts had been wrong. Lucas had been entirely innocent.

"Hey, Zoey," Kate called, returning to the foyer. "You don't have to go. You can wait around with me until Lucas gets back. I'd love the company."

Kate was still wearing Lucas's sweatshirt, and Zoey couldn't help cringing each time she looked at the red-haired girl.

"No, thanks," she said as she opened the door. "Just let Lucas know I stopped by."

She may as well drop the friendly act, Zoey thought. *I know Kate wants Lucas.*

During the course of the past hour, Claire had decided that *Cosmopolitan* was the worst-written publication she'd ever laid eyes on. She would have decided it was the worst-written publication on the newsstand, but she then remembered all of the *Car and Driver*-type magazines that had been on the other end of the rack when she'd purchased the February issue of *Cosmo* before getting on the ferry that afternoon.

She'd bought the thing for its article "Ten Secrets to the Perfect Valentine's Seduction," but the piece had been disappointingly bland. Who needed a magazine to suggest a candlelit bubble bath? Or treating your lover to a massage complete with body oil? The whole article was just further proof that most people in the world were severely lacking in the imagination department.

Still, she had to admit she'd gotten a kick out of buying the magazine. But then again, she would get a kick out of almost anything that related to her Valentine's Day plans with Aaron.

Claire closed the magazine and got up from her bed. As she headed toward her backpack, which lay in the corner of her room, Claire was suddenly aware that her floor was vibrating. Nina's stereo was on so loud that the bass line was pulsing through the house. Claire threw her door open and headed downstairs to have the usual "Nina, can you please turn down your awful music?" discussion.

After pounding on her sister's door five times, the music finally died down. Claire heard the click of

Nina's deadbolt as her sister's door opened a crack.

"Nina," she began, "is it really necessary—" But Claire stopped short in the middle of her sentence. Nina's cheeks were flushed, and her eyes were red and puffy. Obviously she'd been crying.

She softened her tone. "Are you okay, Nina?"

"I'll turn the music down, Claire. You can go back to your cave." Nina began to push the door shut.

"Wait a minute," Claire said, blocking the door with her hand. "What's wrong?"

Nina rolled her eyes. "Take a guess, Claire."

"I thought things were getting back to normal," Claire said gently. "I mean, Benjamin called last night, and he went to school. What happened?"

"Well, I thought things were getting better, too. But that was just wishful thinking."

Wishful thinking on everyone's part, Claire realized. That morning she'd been pleased to see Nina acting like her old strange self. It had meant that Claire didn't have to worry about Nina anymore and was free to concentrate on her own happiness with Aaron. Now Claire felt almost guilty for imagining that anything could be resolved so easily.

"What happened?"

"Nothing. He's still depressed. He's still not himself. And I'm beginning to wonder if he'll ever go back to being the old Benjamin again."

Claire was fairly certain that something had transpired between Nina and Benjamin, but she decided not to push it. The details of what had gotten Nina so upset this time were unimportant.

What mattered was what they could do about it. There had to be a way Claire could help, and the sooner she did something, the sooner she could get back to thinking about her plans with Aaron.

"Do you have any plans for Valentine's Day?" she asked Nina.

"Believe it or not, Claire, I've had other things on my mind."

"I realize that, which is why I brought it up to begin with." Nina's sarcasm wasn't making this any easier. "I'm meeting Aaron at a big party in Portland Friday night. Why don't you and Benjamin come along?"

The look on Nina's face was one of utter confusion. "I don't know . . ."

"Getting off the island might lift Benjamin's spirits," Claire argued. "Besides, what harm could it do?"

"What's in it for you?"

"You may not realize this, Nina, but I don't enjoy seeing you mope around the house."

Nina sighed. "I don't know," she said. "It's not like we have any other plans."

"Good." Claire felt a smile form on her face. "Then you'll come."

"I'll ask Benjamin," Nina responded.

"Great," Claire said, turning to head back up to her room. This good-Samaritan stuff felt surprisingly nice. She climbed the stairs to her room with a spring in her step.

Claire was still patting herself on the back a few minutes later when she realized that her do-gooding might have put a snag in her own plans. Now she'd be stuck chauffeuring Nina and Benjamin back to the island instead of spending the night in the hotel with Aaron.

She knocked on Nina's door yet again.

"While you're at it," Claire said, "why don't you invite Zoey and Lucas along?"

LUCAS

What is love?

I hope you're not expecting some deep philosophical answer to that question, because if you are, you've asked the wrong guy.

I mean, I do know what love is. It's what I feel for Zoey. But when I think about exactly what it is that I feel for her, that's when things get sort of complicated.

Of course, there's the usual physical attraction stuff which I definitely have for Zoey. But I'm trying to keep it cool on that end of things these days, so it's probably best that I don't go on and on about why I really want Zoey. Really, really want her.

Then there's the part of me that would do anything to make her happy (which is why I've been taking so many cold showers lately). And the part that's

Always happier when she's around.

But there's another part, too, and I don't know if she's even aware of it. I think it's something like a mix of gratitude and hope. Part of me always thought of Zoey as this symbol of goodness. I never thought she was perfect or anything, but she was always the kindest person I knew. During the years I was in Youth Authority, surrounded by guys who were the opposite of kind (And that's putting it lightly), just the mental image of Zoey's smile got me through. And when I came back and she actually wanted to be with me, it made me feel like maybe there was a part of me that could be a good person, too. Zoey was the first person who made me feel like I was worth something.

I guess you could say that by loving her I kind of learned to love myself. Which is actually kind of philosophical after all.

Fourteen

The sign at the end of the hall was huge. Lucas couldn't help but stop and stare at it. It read:

Valentine's Carnations!!!
Support the Student Council and Show
Someone You Care!
White = Friendship
Pink = Maybe More
Red = Passion!
Express Valentine's Day Delivery
On Sale Today (Tuesday) and Tomorrow
(Wednesday) in the Cafeteria

Lucas didn't need the sign to remind him he had less than four days to come up with something special to give Zoey for Valentine's Day. Something along with the carnation he was now practically obliged to buy.

"Trying to decide on a color, Cabral?" Jake's voice boomed from behind him.

"More like a gift. Thanks to good old student government, flowers will no longer cut it."

"What about a box of chocolates?"

"Won't exactly score me points for originality," Lucas commented.

"Well, you could say you were going traditional," Jake offered.

There had been a time when Lucas couldn't imagine having a conversation with Jake McRoyan that didn't end in a fistfight. Especially not a conversation that involved Lucas's relationship with Zoey. But now things were different. Spending an evening on the bathroom floor with a drunken Lara McAvoy, who'd been hurling insults and vomit, was enough to make anyone bury the hatchet.

"I doubt that I could say anything that would make up for the lameness if I showed up at Zoey's door with a Whitman Sampler. Girls take this stuff pretty seriously."

"Tell me about it." Jake nodded.

"So, do you have any plans this Friday?" Lucas raised an eyebrow suggestively.

"Actually, I do," Jake said, looking down at his feet.

"You're not still seeing Lara, are you?" Lucas knew the two of them had some kind of on-again, off-again deal going, but as much as he felt sorry for her, Lucas couldn't shake the feeling that Lara was bad news. Especially for someone like Jake, who was trying so hard to stay clean.

"No," Jake said emphatically, "that's over for good this time. I caught her on a bender last week and told her I'd had it."

"Probably a good move," Lucas said.

"Yeah." Jake looked away into the distance. "But maybe we should keep that between us. I wouldn't want to get her in trouble with her father."

Lucas nodded. Normally Lucas didn't like to keep

secrets. They had a funny way of coming back to bite him in the nose. But since he knew Zoey suspected that Lara was up to her usual destructive behavior anyway, he figured that this one was no big deal.

"So if they don't involve Lara McAvoy, what are your Valentine's plans?" Lucas asked.

"Oh, nothing, really. Just going to a meeting and grabbing some dinner with a friend."

Lucas wondered what kind of meeting was held on Friday nights, but then he remembered that meeting was code for AA.

"That sounds about as romantic as my night's gonna be if I don't get some inspiration soon," Lucas mumbled.

"You can bring Zoey along if you want," Jake joked as he headed off down the hall, "They serve coffee in the back."

"I'm broke enough to be tempted," Lucas called after him.

The sad thing was, it was true. As it was, Lucas could barely afford the roses he'd planned on getting Zoey before the whole carnation sale had killed that idea. He could get her perfume, but it would have to be a cheap brand, and that was hardly worth it. And any jewelry he could afford was bound to be a piece of junk.

As he headed down the hall to history class, Lucas was struck by an inspiration. He could make her a romantic candlelit dinner. It was inexpensive but thoughtful—the perfect gift.

There's only one problem, Lucas thought as he took his seat. *I have three days to learn how to cook.*

"I can't decide which is more depressing," Aisha groaned over lunch, "the fact that I have no one to send me a carnation or the fact that it's sloppy joe day.''

Ever since the signs were hung up after homeroom, the halls of Weymouth High had been abuzz with carnation fever. It served as yet another means to remind Aisha of her Christopher-less status.

''One thing you can say for sloppy joes,'' Zoey said as she tried to keep the inside of her sandwich from falling out of its bun, ''at least the name fits.''

''I can think of a few names that are more appropriate. Disgusting joe. Revolting joe.'' Nina paused a moment.

''I can't wait for this one.'' Aisha rolled her eyes.

''Health-inspection-challenged joe.''

''Not bad,'' Aisha said, nodding. ''Then I guess being flowerless is the more depressing one.''

''How do you know you're not going to get one?'' Zoey asked. ''You could have a secret admirer.''

Aisha flashed Zoey a quizzical look. ''Yeah. And I could win the lottery, too, I suppose.''

''I'd put the two at about the same odds,'' Nina said between bites.

''Thanks for the vote of confidence, Nina.''

''If it's any consolation to you, Aisha, I don't expect any flowers this year, either,'' Claire commented.

''Thanks, Claire, but that's only because your boyfriend doesn't go to school here.''

Claire shrugged. ''Carnations aren't even good flowers, anyway. They're barely a notch above baby's breath.''

''All I know is that I can't wait until Friday is over and Cupid leaves the building,'' Aisha grumbled. ''All of this love stuff is getting depressing.''

''You're still coming to the mall with us after

school, though, right?" Zoey's brow was furrowed in concern.

Aisha couldn't blame her. Being alone with the Geiger sisters was never pretty.

"Yeah, I'm still in," Aisha said, "as long as all three of you promise not to be annoyingly happy."

"That shouldn't be too hard," Nina said grimly.

For a moment none of them spoke. They each knew the reason for Nina's comment—Benjamin had failed to come to school yet again. They'd talked the subject to death on the ferry that morning; what else was left to say?

"Is everyone coming to the party on Friday?" Claire broke the silence.

"The one in Portland?" Zoey asked. "Who's throwing it?"

"Someone Aaron knows from boarding school," Claire said. "You're coming, right? You don't mind that he'll be there, do you?"

"Why should I mind?" Zoey said, her tone a bit defensive. "He's your boyfriend."

"Yeah," Nina piped up, "and after all, he's practically family."

Aisha looked at Claire for a response, but as usual, the girl was as cool as a cucumber.

"So you're all coming?" she asked, barely missing a beat.

"Not me," Aisha said. "I have to study. Besides, seeing all those people having fun would only remind me that I'm alone on Valentine's Day."

Claire reached over and put her arm around Aisha. "Don't worry," she said. "You'll find love when you least expect it."

Aisha did a double take. She looked across the table at Zoey, whose surprised expression matched Aisha's thoughts. They must have put something in Claire's sloppy joe.

A Valentine's Trip to the Mall: What They Bought

Claire

After deciding that a garter belt was too overt, purchased a purple silk nightie from Victoria's Secret.

Aisha

Thought the antique pocket watch seemed too extravagant, given the fact that she and Christopher had probably broken up. Settled on a nice (but not too romantic) card.

Nina

Asked the guy at Musicland for jazz CDs that were not too depressing, if there was such a thing. Hoped *Big Bands' Greatest Numbers* and Dave Brubeck's *Time Out* fit the bill.

Zoey

Bought a green sweater from the Gap. Thought that with any luck, Kate would keep her hands off it.

Fifteen

Benjamin sat on the ferry bench trying to drown out his thoughts by listening to Elvis Costello with his Walkman volume on ten. Unfortunately, it wasn't working.

It had been a humiliating day at school. *He'd confused the days of the week* and followed his Wednesday schedule instead of the Thursday one. For second period Benjamin had thought he was going to English but found himself sitting in his English classroom listening to a trig lecture. Worse than his initial confusion was the fact that no one had said anything to him about it. They had all felt too sorry for him or too afraid of embarrassing him. Getting up in the middle of class had been one of the most mortifying *experiences of Benjamin's life*, but he supposed it was the price he paid for missing school and letting one day blend into the next.

Benjamin felt someone sit down next to him on the bench. The mixture of peach shampoo and tobacco told him it was Nina and that she was sucking on a cigarette. He debated turning down the sound on his Walkman, knowing that it would be an invitation for a conversation. Benjamin was definitely not in the mood to chat.

The tap on his shoulder took the decision out of his hands. As usual, Nina wanted to talk. Benjamin had been a fool to think she was sitting next to him for any other reason. He pressed the stop button.

"Hi, Nina," he said.

"Hi, yourself," she replied. "What were you listening to?"

"Punch the Clock," he answered.

"Elvis Costello, huh? I should have brought my double jack."

Nina was referring to the discovery they'd made on their first trip to Boston General, when Benjamin had gotten approved for what would turn out to be useless surgery. After years of disagreeing about music, the two realized that there was one artist they both liked— Elvis Costello. It was far from the only special moment they'd shared on that trip. They had lost their virginity together that night in room 428 of the Malibu Hotel. Now it seemed as though it had been a million years ago. Looking back on it, Benjamin felt as if the whole thing had happened to a different person. A person who was full of hope for his future.

"So, how was your day?" Nina asked in the forced-cheerful tones that Benjamin had come to expect from her.

"Honestly, Nina," he began, "you don't want to know."

"What do you mean, I don't want to know? Of course I want to know. I wouldn't have asked you otherwise."

"Okay, you want to know. But I don't feel like talking about it."

"Oh," she replied shortly. "Well, if it's because you're behind from missing school, I could come home with you and read to you. I don't have much homework, and that way you could start catching up.''

A mixture of emotions stirred in the pit of Benjamin's stomach—frustration, annoyance, even anger, and then guilt. He knew that Nina was concerned, and he hated himself for being irritated with her. But why couldn't she just stop pushing him?

"No, thanks," he replied, making sure to remove any trace of emotion from his voice. "I think I've had enough school for one day."

"No argument here," Nina responded. "Have you decided about tomorrow yet? I think the party sounds like it could be fun."

For some strange reason Nina had gotten it into her head that they should accompany Claire to a party in Portland. Benjamin had told her he'd think about it, but there was no way he wanted to attend. Negotiating his way through a strange house packed with people he didn't know was certainly not Benjamin's idea of a good time.

"Then you should go," he told her.

"I don't want to go if you're not going," she said.

"Then don't go. Suit yourself." There was no point in arguing. Nina could make her own decisions.

"Benjamin, I'm not going to the party without you. Don't you know what tomorrow is?"

"Friday," he said. The mix-up with English had at least drilled the days of the week into his head.

"No. I mean the date," Nina said. Her tone conveyed a hint of frustration.

The truth was that Benjamin had no idea. He hoped it wasn't some kind of anniversary or something. He'd never figured Nina for the type of girl who kept track of those things.

"I give up," Benjamin said with a shrug.

"It's Valentine's Day, Benjamin," Nina replied.

Instantly Benjamin felt a tide of remorse wash over him. He'd had so much on his mind lately, he'd had no idea. He didn't deserve Nina, he thought. She'd been doing everything to try to help him out, and he hadn't even had the decency to remember Valentine's Day. He was blind, bitter, and a horrible boyfriend to boot.

"I'm sorry I forgot, Nina," he began, "but I really don't feel up to a whole celebration these days."

"I understand," Nina said, taking his arm. "I don't care about the stupid party. We can stay home and watch bad Friday night television again for all I care. The important thing is that we're together."

Benjamin sighed. Why should she have to sit with him in silence for another whole evening? Why couldn't she understand that he was damaged, an empty shell with nothing to offer? He could only bring her down.

"I appreciate the thought, Nina, but why don't you just go and have fun? I don't think I'm going to be such great company."

"Benjamin—" she began.

"Really." Benjamin's tone was firm. "Just go."

When she got home, Nina headed straight for the freezer and the pint of Ben & Jerry's she knew it contained. She'd watched countless Richard Simmons infomercials about how using food as a source of emotional comfort was a bad pattern to fall into, but Richard Simmons was a total freak, and ice cream tasted good. Besides, there was nothing else she could do.

Nina wasn't hurt that Benjamin had forgotten Valentine's Day. She wasn't even surprised. When Aisha had complained that she wasn't going to get any carnations, Nina had fought the urge to commiserate; somehow saying it made it all the more true. It was going to be her first Valentine's Day with an actual boyfriend, but Nina felt more alone than she ever had when she was unattached.

In years past she'd always felt free to turn the whole thing into a joke. Zoey would be walking down the hall with her flowers or her candy or whatever cheesy, unoriginal gift Jake had given her, and Nina hadn't felt even a tinge of jealousy. Flowers died, half of those candies had disgusting pink filling, and besides, who'd want a mushy gift from Jake, anyway?

But Nina knew that this year her feelings would be different. Zoey and Lucas would be even cuter than usual. Claire would be nauseatingly excited about seeing Aaron. Even Aisha, whose romantic status with Christopher would make her comparably depressed, would be studying in the library and therefore of no use to Nina. Meanwhile, Benjamin would be off sitting in his black hole of depression. Even if Cupid packed an extra-strength arrow, she doubted it could get Benjamin in the spirit.

Maybe he was right, Nina thought as she scarfed down another spoonful of Chunky Monkey. *Maybe I should just go to the party*. Given Benjamin's recent preference for being alone, he'd probably want her to be in Portland, even if it was supposed to be the most romantic night of the year.

Just when Nina thought she couldn't get more depressed, Claire entered the kitchen. She was wearing the same cheerful grin she'd had on all week.

"Good afternoon, Nina," Claire said perkily. Nina wondered whether Sarah Mendel's happy disease was contagious and hoped that she was immune.

"Claire, you're gonna have to turn it down a

notch,'' Nina grumbled. "I'm trying to drown my sorrows in ice cream, and the rays of sunshine you're emanating could cause it to melt.''

Claire's smile faded at her sister's words. She furrowed her brow in what Nina recognized as Claire's new concerned face.

"Are you okay, Nina?'' Claire asked, taking a seat at the table.

"Just peachy. Thanks for asking.'' Even if her sister had decided to switch personalities, Nina wanted to remain her same sarcastic self.

"Nina, what is it?''

Nina let out an exasperated sigh. Claire would find out sooner or later, as everyone on the island would.

"Benjamin doesn't want to go to the party tomorrow,'' she said. "In fact, he doesn't really want to do anything. I had to tell him it was Valentine's Day tomorrow.''

Claire nodded. "So what are you going to do?''

"I have no idea. Benjamin says I should go to the party without him.''

Claire shrugged. "Maybe you should.''

"It's not that simple, Claire,'' Nina began. "It's not just about tomorrow night. I want Benjamin to let me help him through this, but all he seems to want is to be rid of me. If I go to the party, it's like I'm just giving up.''

"Maybe you should just give up, then.''

"Benjamin and I have something special, Claire. I can't just walk away from him when he's in so much pain.''

"I'm not suggesting that you just walk away. All I'm saying is that Benjamin is going through a lot right now.''

"You don't think I realize that?''

"I know you do. But maybe no one can really understand what Benjamin is feeling. Maybe he needs to work it out on his own."

"So you're saying I should do what he says? That I should leave him alone and depressed and do absolutely nothing to try to help him out of it?"

"I don't think you have much of a choice, Nina."

Nina felt the tears well up in her eyes. Even if her sister was right, Nina knew there was no way she could do what Claire suggested. Maybe Claire could walk away from someone she loved. After all, she *was* the ice princess.

But Benjamin meant too much to Nina for her to let him go through this alone. And even if he couldn't show it now, Nina knew she meant the same to him.

Sixteen

After dinner Claire headed out to the Passmores' house. The situation with Benjamin was taking its toll on Nina, and Claire was determined to help resolve it. She was sure that Benjamin sensed the hell he was putting his girlfriend through. She was also pretty certain that Nina had yet to make her feelings clear to Benjamin.

Someone had to alert Benjamin to the effects his actions were having on Nina, and Claire knew she was the only one who could get through to him.

Claire let out an involuntary shiver as she waited for someone to answer the door. Although it was another clear night, the temperature must have dropped twenty degrees since sunset.

"Claire." Zoey's surprise was evident in her voice. "What brings you here?"

Zoey was right to be surprised. Since she and Benjamin had broken up, Claire hadn't exactly been a regular at the Passmores'. Even when they had been a couple, Claire had always preferred the unobtrusive privacy of her room to the homey, anyone-could-knock-at-any-time feeling of the Passmores'. But that night the circumstances called for Claire to visit Benjamin on his turf. What she had to say couldn't be said on the phone.

"I'm here to see Benjamin, actually," Claire said, flashing a smile to undercut the oddness of her statement.

"Oh." As usual, Zoey's thoughts were written all over her face. Claire's visit had thrown her for a loop. One of these days that girl would have to learn the art of artifice.

"Can I come in?" Claire asked, shivering slightly in the cold air.

"Yeah, sure. Um, Benjamin's in his room, but I don't know if he's really in the mood for visitors."

"Well, I'll just have to try my luck, then," Claire said, taking off her coat and hanging it on the coatrack. As she headed toward Benjamin's room she was aware of Zoey's presence behind her.

"I remember the way, Zoey. Thanks, though." Claire turned back around and rolled her eyes. If she'd been there for almost any other purpose, Claire would have gotten some amusement from rattling Zoey. But as it was, she couldn't even enjoy the little mischief she'd made. Too much was at stake.

She took a deep breath and knocked on Benjamin's door.

"Who's there?" he called from the other side of the door.

He doesn't recognize my knock anymore, Claire noted. "It's Claire, Benjamin. Can I talk to you for a minute?"

There was a pause. "Come on in."

She opened the door and stepped into his room. It was exactly how she remembered it. Same wall of CDs. Same upside-down posters hanging on the walls. The only things that were different since the last time

Claire had been there were the two of them—or were they?

"What brings you here, Claire?" Benjamin asked from behind those dark, impenetrable Ray-Bans. He sat on his bed, facing the general direction of the door.

"What do you think, Benjamin?" Claire asked, figuring it was better to feel him out before diving into uncharted waters.

"I'd say it was the Ghost of Valentine's Day Past, but I think that's the wrong holiday."

"It's nice to see you still have your sense of humor," she said, seating herself on his desk chair.

"Even if I'm still missing my sight?" Benjamin asked, giving Claire the first taste of a bitterness she'd not yet witnessed for herself. He really had changed.

"Even if you haven't been yourself recently."

"So is that what this is, Claire? A get-well visit?"

"In part, I guess," she answered. "Benjamin, I want you to know how sorry I am that the operation didn't go your way."

"Well, Claire, I appreciate your condolences. It's always heartening to know that the good folk of Chatham Island pity me."

Claire let out a chuckle. "Benjamin, you're about the only person on this island whom I *don't* pity."

"And why's that?"

"Because everyone else around here walks around in some little dream world of their own creation. They all see things the way they want them to be. You see them the way they are. We're alike in that way."

"But you forget, Claire. I don't *see* things at all."

Claire let out a sigh. "Yes, you do, Benjamin, and you know it. And even if you don't want to realize it now, you can still see in the way that really matters."

"That's very touching," Benjamin said tonelessly.

"Well, maybe you'll think about it sometime. But that's not what I came here to tell you."

"I'm all ears."

"Even though you are understandably upset, Benjamin, you shouldn't put Nina through this. It isn't fair to her."

For the first time since she'd entered the room, Claire detected feeling in Benjamin's face. It seemed to soften at the mention of her sister's name.

"Nina's not like us, Benjamin. She's an emotional person, and she can't see the big picture. Everything hits her on a gut level. She may put up a brave front, but everything you dish out she takes personally. Even if you don't mean to do it, Benjamin, that's the effect you're having on her."

Neither one of them said anything for a moment. Finally Benjamin broke the silence.

"I understand your meaning," he said.

"I knew you would." She rose to leave. Now that Nina was taken care of, she could concentrate her energies where they really belonged—on Aaron.

"You know, Lucas," Kate said, "you could have just doubled the recipe and warmed it up tomorrow."

"No way," Lucas protested. "That would be like cheating or something."

He had spent the better part of the past two hours trying to perfect the recipe for marinara sauce with basil that he'd found in one of his mother's cookbooks. So far, the key ingredient had been the carrots, which Kate had told him to add to cut the acidity of the crushed tomatoes. But he still had to let it simmer for five more minutes until he and Kate could test the final product.

"Does Zoey know how lucky she is to have a guy

like you?'' Kate asked. "Most guys barely remember Valentine's Day, much less spend all this time learning to cook a romantic dinner. Believe me, I know this for a fact.''

"Actually, I'm the lucky one. Zoey is the best thing that ever happened to me. She practically turned my life around.''

Kate put up a hand in mock protest. "Stop. You're getting too sweet and romantic. You're going to set my standards for guys too high.''

"You're the one who'd better cut it out,'' Lucas answered with a laugh. "If you give me too big an ego, Zoey'll never forgive you.''

"I'll bet,'' Kate mumbled.

Lucas stopped stirring the sauce. "What does that mean?''

"Nothing, really,'' Kate replied. "I just get the feeling that Zoey doesn't like me too much.''

"What?''

"I don't know why, but I just get a weird vibe from her. Has she said something to you about it? You can tell me the truth. I won't be hurt.''

"She hasn't said a word about you, Kate,'' Lucas answered. It was the absolute truth. Come to think of it, Zoey had barely expressed an opinion about Kate one way or the other since they'd first met. "But we all had a good time last weekend.''

"Oh, it's not that,'' Kate said. "She was perfectly cordial and nice. I just don't think we exactly bonded.''

"She's just been preoccupied,'' Lucas reasoned. "There's a lot of stuff going on with her brother right now. I'm sure that's why she didn't seem all there.''

"That must be it.'' Kate nodded. "From everything you've said about her, I feel like I'm missing out.

When things settle down for her, I'd really like to get to know her better."

"I'm sure she'd like that, too," Lucas said.

Zoey knocked on her brother's door and awaited his response. From inside she could hear a saxophone wailing loudly. Maybe he hadn't heard her knock. She raised her hand to rap again but was stopped by the sudden opening of the door.

"What is it, Zoey?" Benjamin asked.

She was taken aback. Benjamin almost never came to the door himself.

"I just wanted to see what was up," she said.

"You mean you wanted to know why Claire came by, right?"

Zoey flushed at the bluntness of his question. But why should she feel guilty about it? Of course she was curious; it wasn't every day that Claire came over at nine o'clock at night to see Benjamin.

"Yeah," Zoey admitted. "What was she doing here?"

"Like everyone else, Claire wanted to see how I was doing and tell me what little reason I have to be upset."

"And she picked tonight to do it?"

"Obviously," Benjamin said.

"Are you sure that's the only reason she came by?" Zoey was still confused. There had to be something more to it. With Claire, there always was.

"What else could there be, Zoey?"

"I don't know," she admitted.

"Is that all, Zo? Because if you don't mind—"

"I know. You'd like to be alone."

Zoey closed the door behind her and went back to the kitchen, where she paced around, wondering what had really transpired between Claire and her brother. Benjamin wouldn't lie to her, but most of the time he liked to keep his personal life private. What could Claire have wanted?

She let out a sigh. Becoming so preoccupied with Claire's visit had made her forget the disappointment she'd felt when she first saw Claire at the door instead of Lucas. Normally it was Lucas who visited in the evenings, but things weren't normal these days. Lucas hadn't stopped by once in the past three nights, and Zoey knew it had something to do with his new house-guest. She looked up at his house to see if any of the lights were still on.

I'll just go over to his house, she decided. That way I can give him a pre-Valentine's kiss.

Zoey threw on her jacket and slipped out the front door, deciding that since her parents' door was already closed, she'd be better off not disturbing them.

As she scampered alongside Lucas's house, Zoey stepped into the glow from his kitchen light. Who could be in the Cabrals' kitchen at this time of night? She knew that she should go directly to the front door and ring the bell. Spying through windows and door-ways had only brought her grief, and she had promised herself to trust Lucas from now on. Still, since she trusted him so completely, there was no harm in look-ing, right?

Zoey peered into the window. Lucas was feeding Kate something on a spoon. It looked like a scene from *Lady and the Tramp*, and Zoey already knew which one of them was the tramp.

Immediately she ran back to her house. As much as she tried to convince herself that there must be a per-fectly logical explanation for the scene she'd just wit-nessed, Zoey couldn't get one thought out of her mind: Could Lucas be falling for Kate's act?

The Carnations
(Who Got What)

ZOEY received three red ones from Lucas. The note read, *Meet me at my house at 6 for your real Valentine's present. I love you. Lucas.*

AISHA received one white one from Zoey. The thought was sweet, but it still brought little consolation.

CLAIRE received no flowers. Big deal.

NINA received two red flowers. One came with a note that read, in Zoey's handwriting. *Love, Benjamin.*

LUCAS received a red one from Zoey. The note read, *Always remember I love you, not just because it's Valentine's Day.—Zoey.*

JAKE received one pink one from Louise.

BENJAMIN wasn't in school, so they gave back to Nina the four red ones she had bought.

Seventeen

Jake sat on the floor of the hallway feeling the cold tile through the denim of his jeans. He leaned his head against the wall, weighing the pros and cons of entering the cafeteria.

On the pro side was eating. Even if the macaroni and cheese was slimy, it was still food. And as his growling stomach could attest, Jake was hungry.

On the con side was the potential for seeing Louise. Jake knew that she had lunch this period, and ever since he'd received the pink carnation she'd sent him, he wasn't sure what to say to her.

He opened the note that had come with the flower and read it yet again. *Let's take our friendship one day at a time. Happy Valentine's Day—Louise.*

No matter how many times he read it, the card's meaning was still a mystery to Jake. The ''one day at a time'' reference from the AA motto was obvious. The ''Happy Valentine's Day'' part was obvious. But what he couldn't figure out was Louise's intention in sending the flower.

After all, Jake reasoned, if Louise's point had been simple friendship, why hadn't she sent him a white carnation? That was the color that was supposed to mean it was just a friendly little Valentine's Day greeting. But the flower in his hand was not white; it was very definitely pink. And unless there had been some strange mix-up in the delivery, that meant Louise had wanted to send quite a different message to Jake. As the signs all over school said, pink equaled "maybe more."

As uncomfortable as it was making him, Jake had to acknowledge that pink was, in reality, the most appropriate color of flower for Louise Kronenberger to have sent him. They had been spending a major amount of time together, even if it was in a room full of other alcoholics. And it was pretty clear that the two of them understood each other in a way that people who weren't going through the program couldn't. Not to mention the long, questionable hug they'd shared after the meeting on Monday. Or the fact that they were having dinner together after that night's meeting, which could be considered a Valentine's Day date.

But then again, it didn't have to be. It could just be two friends from AA going to dinner together on a Friday night because they both had no other plans.

If only Jake knew which one it was.

If only he knew which one he wanted it to be.

Jake smiled ruefully. If someone would have told him two months before that he'd be spending Valentine's Day with Louise Kronenberger, he would have thought they were off their rocker. It was funny how quickly things—and people, for that matter—could change.

"Hey, Jake." The sound of Zoey's voice ripped Jake from his thoughts and brought him back to earth.

Speaking of things changing, weren't you supposed to be my Valentine once? he thought. "Hi, Zoey."

"What are you doing out here?" she asked. "The

macaroni and cheese isn't *that* frightening, is it?"

"Actually, I was just deciding whether to brave it or head out to McDonald's." It was partially the truth, anyway. "What are *you* doing out here? Shouldn't you be in there holding your daily conference of Chatham Island girls?" The fact that lunchtime had always been girls-only had been a sore spot for Jake while he and Zoey were together. What did they have to talk about that they couldn't say around guys? And why did they have to do it every day?

"Just taking a quick bathroom break," Zoey replied. She motioned to the flower in his hand. "Who's that from, if you don't mind my asking?"

"Nobody. Just a friend," Jake responded. It was sort of the truth, and he didn't exactly want to get into a discussion with Zoey about his new friendship or whatever it was. He knew there was no love lost between Zoey and Louise.

"I don't know, Jake," Zoey said as she walked down the hall in the direction of the girls' room. Even from a distance, he could detect the hint of a teasing twinkle in her blue eyes. "Doesn't pink mean 'maybe more'?"

"With emphasis on the *maybe*," Jake called back to her.

Seeing Zoey had helped him make up his mind. McDonald's it was. If he went into the cafeteria, there were bound to be more questions. He might as well bide his time and see how things with Louise went that night.

Aisha gingerly entered her locker combination with trembling fingers. Getting back her physics quiz last period had been enough to chase away her Valentine's Day blues. She had gotten a 99.5, with the half point deduction due to a forgotten negative sign. It still wasn't as great as getting a Valentine's Day card from Christopher would have been, but Aisha was happy to take what she could get.

She tossed her physics notebook onto her locker shelf with a sense of satisfaction. All of her studying had paid off. Aisha was confident that she was well on her way to the Westinghouse scholarship.

Maybe she could even reward herself by taking the night off from studying and heading down to the party in Portland with Zoey and Lucas. It would be nice to feel like an actual teenager again. And who knew— maybe there'd be a cute guy there who would take her mind off missing Christopher. Why not? It had been a pretty lucky Valentine's Day so far.

"How'd you do on the quiz?"

Aisha knew that the self-satisfied tone could be coming from only one source. She turned and saw David Barnes leaning against the locker next to hers. Hoping for a Barnes-free day, she'd made a quick getaway after class ended. So much for her lucky streak.

"I'm very satisfied with my grade, David. Thanks for your concern." Aisha made sure to match his self-assurance with her own sarcasm.

"Well, add that to the list of things we have in common, then," he said, using his right hand to straighten his glasses. His every gesture dripped with the excess of his huge ego. "But how could I not be satisfied with my score? One hundred is pretty good when there's no extra credit."

Of course he'd stopped by to gloat about his perfect score. Aisha made sure that her facial expression hid the fact that David had actually done better than she had. It was only half a point. She'd practically gotten a perfect score herself. Practically.

What a jerk he is, she said to herself. ''If that's all you dropped by for, David,'' Aisha remarked as she fumbled through her locker with pointed disinterest, ''I've got to get ready for next period.'' *In other words, get lost.*

''Actually, there is another matter,'' he said vaguely.

Aisha turned to face him, bracing herself for whatever he was going to dish out. To her great surprise, David pulled his left hand out from behind his back. In it was a single white carnation.

''What's that for?'' Aisha asked, not even bothering to hide her surprise.

''Just to show you it's a friendly competition,'' David said, handing her the flower.

''Thanks.'' Her tone was still one of confusion. Could David actually be nice after all?

''And to show you that I won't be a sore winner,'' he added, his blue eyes shining in triumph.

He thinks he's so damn clever, Aisha fumed. For a minute she'd been stupid enough to entertain the possibility that David could actually act like a human being. It was a mistake she didn't intend ever to make again.

In a single motion she crumpled up the flower and threw it back in his face.

''You're right about one thing,'' Aisha called over her shoulder as she turned and stomped down the hall. ''You won't be a sore winner. You won't be a winner at all.''

Aisha knew that there was no way she could go to the party now. She couldn't reward herself yet. First she had to study. Then she had to ensure she wouldn't make any more careless mistakes.

This is the last time I let David Barnes beat me, she vowed. *Next time I'll be the one with the perfect score.*

JAKE

To be honest, I have no idea what love is, other than the love you have for your family, which is probably not what you're asking about.

The truth is, I think I have a better grasp on lust. There was Claire. I thought I cared about her, but the more I think about it, the more I realize that our relationship was about her wanting who-knows-what and me thinking she was the best-looking girl I'd ever seen. Then there was homecoming night with Louise, which was lust mixed with booze and cocaine. And finally there was Lara. Part of me felt sorry for her and wanted to help her out, but if I hadn't been getting laid, I doubt it would have taken me so long to figure out that she was truly bad news.

The only person I would say I even came close to being in love with was Zoey. In fact, I was pretty sure that what we had was love. But it couldn't have been if she could fall for Lucas so quickly.

So, as I said, on the subject of love, I'm pretty clueless.

Eighteen

The sun had started to fade by the time Jake made his second loop around the island. He had decided to burn off some nervous energy by going for a jog but guessed by the sun's angle that he might now be running late. His meeting started at seven, but he still had to shower, change, and get on the ferry. Not wanting to shell out the extra money for the water taxi, he quickened the pace of his run.

Finally Jake opened the sliding door that led directly into his room. The combination of the cold winter air and his sweat had made his clothes oddly clammy. Within seconds Jake managed to peel them off, throw a towel around his waist, and hit the shower down the hall.

As he lathered his muscular chest, Jake considered what he would wear. Should he play it totally casual, as he would if he were only going to an AA meeting and not out to dinner afterward? Or should he dress up a little, as he would if he were going out on a date?

This is way too complicated, Jake thought as he rinsed himself and turned off the water.

Jake had managed to avoid Louise for the entire school day, which he felt was a good thing. First of all, he had started to feel a little guilty for not buying her a flower. Whatever was going to happen between them, it would have been a nice thing to do.

But the real reason he'd made a point of dodging Louise had been his own confusion over the status of things between them. It would have been too hard to get a good read off her in the hall between classes. There wasn't anybody, except maybe Claire, who wasn't naturally stressed out and frazzled in the middle of the school day. Whatever was going to happen between Jake and Louise had to be resolved that night, one way or the other.

Jake opened his closet door and took out a pair of jeans and his navy J. Crew roll-neck sweater. It was, he reasoned, an outfit that could go either way.

May as well keep things up in the air, Jake figured as he closed the door and tossed the clothes onto his bed. Jake did a double take. He thought he'd seen something out of the corner of his eye just as he'd tossed the clothing. Something lying on his otherwise neatly made bed. It was now covered by the sweater. Still in his towel, he decided to check it out.

Jake lifted the sweater from his bed to find a heart-shaped candy box like the ones he remembered having given Zoey in the past. Only instead of being red or pink, the way those things usually were, this one had been painted a sinister black.

Jake opened the box to find the candies inside half eaten and squished. It was totally disgusting. On top of the candies was a note, which Jake unfolded and read. It said:

Like it or not, I'm still your Valentine. Lara.

An involuntary shudder passed through Jake's body, and it wasn't because he was still in his wet towel. As she'd probably intended, Lara's Valentine's Day "gift" had freaked Jake out. He suddenly felt as though he were trapped in the movie *Fatal Attraction*, with Lara cast in the Glenn Close role. But Lara wasn't that crazy, was she?

Jake had the sinking feeling he was about to find out.

"This is the best linguine I've ever had," Zoey said as she took another bite. "When did you learn to cook like this, Lucas?"

"Last night," Lucas answered as he wiped the corners of his mouth with a napkin. "Are you sure the sauce isn't too heavy on the basil?"

"Everything is perfect," she said, reaching across the candlelit table to hold his hand. "This is truly the best Valentine's Day present I've ever gotten."

"Well, I have to admit that I got some help from Kate."

So that was what she'd witnessed the previous night. She tried to dismiss the wave of irritation that swept over her when she thought of Kate helping with the meal. After all, Lucas had planned this romantic Valentine's Day dinner for no one but Zoey.

"Have I told you lately how lucky I am to have you for a boyfriend?" Zoey asked.

"Not in the last ten minutes," Lucas replied with a semisheepish grin.

"I love you," she said, kissing his hand. "Thank you again for this wonderful meal."

"As much as I'd love to stay here and get thanked all night, we'd better get a move on if we're gonna make the eight o'clock ferry," Lucas said, rising to clear the dishes.

Between the ferry ride, the time it took to get to the garage in Weymouth where the Passmores' van was parked, and the hourlong drive to Portland, Zoey and

Lucas expected to arrive at the party around ten o'clock, just when things would be in full swing.

Zoey got up also. "I think I'll put in one final call to Benjamin. Maybe by some miracle he's changed his mind about coming."

"It can't hurt to call," Lucas said, shrugging. "While you're at it, I'm going to go upstairs and put on my new sweater."

Zoey smiled as she headed toward the kitchen phone. Even if he was only doing it to humor her, Zoey was happy that Lucas had liked her gift enough to put it on right away. If only Benjamin would cheer up a little, it would be the perfect Valentine's Day.

"Hey, Benjamin," Zoey said when she heard her brother's voice on the other end of the line. He had answered the phone instead of letting the machine get it, which Zoey took to be a good sign.

"Shouldn't you be on your way to Portland about now?"

"Yeah," she answered, "we're just about to leave for the ferry. I just wanted to make sure you hadn't changed your mind about coming. I'm sure it's gonna be fun."

She could hear Benjamin's sigh across the phone line. "I don't think so, Zo. But thanks for asking."

"Okay," she said, trying not to sound disappointed. "Well, have fun with Nina."

"Okay," he said. "Bye."

"No luck?" Lucas asked. He had changed into the green Gap sweater, which, Zoey noted, made his eyes look even better than she'd thought it would.

"Nope," she responded. "But at least he was with it enough to answer the phone."

"That's a good sign," Lucas said hopefully.

"I guess so," Zoey agreed. Looking at the clock, she added, "We'd better get going."

"You know," Lucas said, putting his arm around her, "I'm almost tempted to blow off this whole party thing and spend the rest of this Valentine's Day showing you how much I love you."

Zoey was enjoying the feeling of being held in Lucas's arms, especially since she'd been there so seldom lately. "Why don't we, then? We aren't even going to know anyone at this party but Claire." Zoey left out Aaron's name on purpose. Why take the chance of putting a damper on Lucas's mood?

"We can't," Lucas said, disengaging himself from her embrace with a peck on the cheek. "I told Kate we'd give her a ride back."

Zoey nearly choked. "*Kate's* coming? Why?"

"I invited her," Lucas said matter-of-factly.

"And I'm sure she was just thrilled to horn in on our Valentine's Day plans," Zoey said sharply.

"What do you mean, horn in on our plans? It's not like she joined us for dinner." Lucas frowned. "She's meeting us at a big party. There'll be a million people there. Why shouldn't Kate be one of them?"

"Whatever." Zoey seethed as she put on her coat. She couldn't believe that Lucas was so naïve. Couldn't he see that Kate was after him?

Nineteen

Benjamin hung up the phone and sat down on his bed, making sure to turn the volume of his stereo back up. He knew Zoey was only trying to help by calling, but he couldn't forget the pity in her voice. It seemed to say, *Poor Benjamin. He can't even come out to a party and have fun anymore.* The worst part was, the sentiment was true.

Why shouldn't Zoey pity him? More and more it was becoming clear that his life was a joke. For years he had worked hard to convince himself and everyone else that it didn't matter that he couldn't see. All of that effort had been put forth for the sole purpose of proving that everything was fine. So what if he was blind? It didn't really matter.

Benjamin laughed aloud at the thought of his own naïveté. Of course it mattered that he was blind! How could it not? Being blind meant that the whole course of his life had to be dictated by everything he couldn't do.

He couldn't pick out his own clothes. He couldn't read the paper. He couldn't go anywhere unfamiliar without someone else around to guide him. Benjamin was going to be forever locked in childhood—in a state of near-total dependence. To pretend anything different was to be in denial, the same denial he'd been in all these years.

The irony was that everyone wanted him to go back to that charade. To resume his role of the blind super-boy, invincible except when it came to any task that required the basic sense of sight.

After Claire's visit, he'd almost convinced himself that that was what he should do. Benjamin knew she was right, that his depression was hurting everyone around him, especially Nina. And Nina was the last person Benjamin wanted to hurt.

All day long he'd tried to build up his resolve for her sake. He'd spent the day cleaning his room, fig-uring it was the first step in restoring the old order to his life. But now, sitting alone in his world of dark-ness, Benjamin knew he could never really go back to the way things had been before the operation. He had lost the will to pretend.

Benjamin was called back from the recesses of his own thoughts by the sound of Ella Fitzgerald's voice: "Sophisticate—sophisticate—sophisticate—sophisti-cate . . ." The CD obviously had a scratch.

It was an annoyance of minor significance compared to the things that occupied his thoughts, yet it stirred something within him. A feeling he'd been trying to suppress for over a month. A feeling so strong, he'd been afraid to let it surface. It was anger.

Benjamin rose from his bed, trying to contain the feeling, which had now taken a firm hold somewhere deep within him.

"Sophisticate—sophisticate—sophisticate—sophis-ticate—sophis—"

"Shut up!" He screamed it so loudly that he could feel the vibrations of his voice throughout the room.

Benjamin grabbed for the desk chair and began

thrashing it in the direction of his stereo with the force of all of the pent-up rage within him. After a few swings, Ella was quieted, but the storm within him had just begun.

Benjamin spun about the room, thinking not only of the darkness and the helplessness but also of the charade as he flailed the chair around with abandon.

He struck out against the doctors who had failed him, the world that pitied him, and the people who wanted him to ignore his blindness all over again. Hearing the sounds of his possessions shattering, he thought of his parents, of Zoey, of Claire—and of Nina. Benjamin knew he was letting them all down. And with a fresh fury he flung the chair as hard as he could into the wall.

"Looks like someone doesn't have a Valentine."

Aisha was tempted to ignore the comment and keep on working, but she decided that would be an incredibly immature way to deal with David. Besides, he'd probably get a kick out of it. And the last thing she wanted was to give him the slightest bit of joy.

"I don't exactly see your sweetheart anywhere," Aisha replied, looking around the nearly empty library.

"Yeah, well, that's different," David said, taking a seat next to her. "I'm a guy."

Aisha made a face. "I won't debate that point with you, but would you mind explaining why it's any worse for me to be here studying on Valentine's Day than it is for you?"

"Well, first of all, Valentine's Day is a sentimental holiday, and guys aren't sentimental. It was practically invented for women's sakes."

"Is that so?" Aisha's tone made it clear that she wasn't buying his explanation.

"Yes, it is. I mean, look at the traditional gifts: candy, flowers. Guys don't want that stuff."

"Whatever gets you through the night, David." Aisha turned back to her work.

"Besides," David continued, "as a guy, I have years left to find my soul mate. But as a woman, you have only a limited window: the period when you still have your good looks. It's a fact that men get better with age and women just get old."

Without looking up from her notebook, Aisha responded with a snort. She knew Claire had been right and that David was simply trying to nettle her. But she really couldn't stand the guy. And he wasn't just annoying; he was a sexist pig to boot.

"You know, David," Aisha said, looking him in the eye, "I just realized something. All this time I thought you were simply afraid of losing to me. Now I see that you can't stand the thought of losing to a female. Maybe you should stop working on your physics and start working on building up your fragile male ego."

Aisha was pleased to see David's blue eyes narrow a bit. For once she'd gotten him good.

Serves him right for being such a jerk, she thought as he got up from his chair.

"What's funny about that, Aisha," David called as he walked back to his study carrel, "is that you think that the thought of your beating me had even crossed my mind. That'll never happen, and you know it as well as I do."

"We'll see," Aisha called back.

She knew he was bluffing. Of course he was worried that she'd beat him out for the Westinghouse scholarship; why would he bother trying to rattle her if he didn't think she could actually win? Aisha turned back to her notes. She was more determined than ever to do just that.

Twenty

Nina sighed as she held up the package containing Benjamin's present. She'd just spent the past twenty minutes trying to wrap up the two CDs she'd bought. Unfortunately, it hadn't exactly worked. The corners were totally uneven, and since she hadn't been able to find clear tape anywhere in the house, the whole thing was held together by big pieces of yellowish masking tape.

Well, at least Benjamin won't know the difference, Nina thought as she bundled up and headed out the door. *There are advantages to having a blind boyfriend.*

As she walked across Lighthouse Road Nina crossed her fingers. She knew Benjamin didn't care about the fact that it was Valentine's Day, but she hoped that he'd at least be in one of his better moods. Maybe her present would cheer him up.

Turning right on Camden, she nearly bumped into Zoey and Lucas.

"Hey, Nina," Lucas said.

"Shouldn't you guys be halfway to Portland by now?" she asked.

"We're on our way," Zoey said. "Benjamin's at home."

"Where else?" Nina made no effort to conceal the glumness in her tone. "By the way, Zoey, thank you for the flower."

"What flower?" Zoey asked, a bit too quickly. "Benjamin asked me to buy it."

Nina gave her a look. "You don't have to pretend. I know that up until yesterday Benjamin had no idea it was Valentine's Day, much less that the student government was torturing all of us with their carnation sale." Nina's expression softened as she saw Zoey blush guiltily. "It was a very sweet thing to do, and I appreciate it."

"Well, I know Benjamin would have gotten you one if he weren't so . . ." Zoey's voice trailed off.

"Yeah," Nina answered. She knew what Zoey had been going to say: *if Benjamin weren't so miserable.*

"I talked to him just now, and he sounded pretty upbeat," Zoey said brightly.

"Well," said Nina with a sigh, "let's hope it lasts."

The first thing Nina was aware of as she entered the Passmores' house was the crashing sound of glass breaking. She rushed to the kitchen, hoping that Benjamin hadn't cut himself on the broken shards. But the kitchen was empty, and the horrible sound continued.

As Nina headed upstairs toward Benjamin's room, the noise grew louder and louder. Benjamin had some taste for atonal music, but this sounded way too real to be coming from his stereo. Nina pounded on Benjamin's door and then flung it open.

The entire place was trashed. Papers were scattered everywhere, as were smashed-up CDs and half-ripped books. The computer monitor lay tilted on the ground, but luckily it wasn't cracked. Nina couldn't say the same for the stereo. In the center of it all stood Benjamin. The chair he held above his head had two cracked legs, and the Ray-Bans he always wore lay shattered on the floor in front of him. A crazed look had replaced the sunglasses on his face. He turned his unseeing eyes in Nina's general direction.

"Benjamin!" she cried.

"Go away, Nina," he spat. "Go away!"

"I'm not leaving, Benjamin. Not until you tell me what you're doing."

"What does it look like, Nina? I'm letting out some stress."

"That qualifies for the understatement of the year," she said.

"Just get out, Nina!"

Nina instantly felt awful about her sarcastic remark. This was obviously not a situation that could be resolved by laughter.

"Benjamin," she said, stepping over the debris to take his hand, "tell me what's wrong. How can I help you through this?"

Benjamin dropped the chair and began to shake. His sobs were audible, and because he was without the Ray-Bans, Nina could see the tears fall from his eyes. The previous week she'd heard him sobbing in the darkness, but Nina had never actually seen Benjamin cry before. It tore at her heart to see him in so much pain.

Nina couldn't keep herself from crying also as she went to hold him. Standing in the middle of Benjamin's destroyed room, both of them sobbing uncontrollably, Nina felt a strange burst of hope. Benjamin was finally letting go—and he was allowing her to be a part of it.

This could be the turning point, not just for Benjamin but for our relationship, she thought.

But all of a sudden Benjamin turned away.

"Nina—"

"Benjamin," she said, "you don't have to feel ashamed around me. I love you. I want to be here for you."

"Nina . . . just . . . please, go away."

"I'm not going anywhere, Benjamin. We're in this together. We've been in it together from the beginning."

"I can't do this anymore, Nina," he said. "I can't drag you down with me."

There was something different about his tone. Something firmer. It was frighteningly calm.

"What are you saying, Benjamin?" she asked, unsure that she wanted to hear the answer.

"I'm saying it's over."

The weight of his words hit Nina like a punch in the gut. She looked into his cold, dead eyes. They were red from crying but showed no other emotion.

"You don't mean that. . . ."

"I mean it, Nina. It's over between us."

Twenty-one

"I wonder if Kate will already be there," Lucas said as he looked out the window.

"I have no idea," Zoey said, making sure to concentrate on the road ahead. She didn't want Lucas to catch the annoyed look on her face. Why in the world had he invited Kate to begin with? And if she had another ride to the party, why did she need them to drive her home?

"All right, Zoey," he said, turning to face her. "Just what is it you have against Kate?"

Just the fact that she obviously wants you and you're too naïve to notice it, Zoey thought. "What makes you ask that?"

"She said something last night that, well, it just makes me wonder."

"What did she say?" Zoey was more interested in the answer than Lucas could possibly imagine. It would give her an insight into Kate's game.

"Kate doesn't think you like her," Lucas replied.

Zoey let out a snort. "And whatever gave her that impression?" Her tone was one of sheer sarcasm. It couldn't have been lost on Lucas.

Out of the corner of her eye, Zoey could see Lucas

looking at her quizzically. "I'm not sure, but I'm starting to think she was on to something."

"I'm surprised you didn't just agree with her all along. After all; she is so smart."

"What is that suppose to mean?" Lucas was indignant. "And what has Kate ever done to you?"

If Lucas wasn't going to catch on, Zoey would alert him to the fact that his houseguest was after more than his hospitality.

"Nothing . . . yet," Zoey replied, "but believe me, she'd like to do something, all right. The only way Kate sees you as a brother is if she's turned on by incest."

"What?" Lucas's tone sounded more outraged than confused. "Where are you coming up with this?"

"Just call it a woman's instinct," Zoey said. "Believe me, I can *tell*."

"Oh, yeah," he said, "like you could *tell* about Aaron Mendel, right?"

Zoey turned away from the road to cast an angry glance at Lucas. He could only be bringing Aaron up for one reason. He'd been flirting with Kate to get back at her, just as he'd done the time he hooked up with Claire to get back at her for talking to Jake.

"No, it's more like the way I could tell you were fooling around with Claire," Zoey spat back.

"Oh, great, Zoey," Lucas said, raising his voice. "Just bring up ancient history. Am I going to have to pay for one stupid mistake for the rest of my life?"

"Yeah," she replied hotly. "The same way you've been making me pay for my mistake with Aaron!"

"Making you pay? Making you pay? I took you back practically without an apology, and meanwhile you still rake me over the coals about Claire any chance you get!"

"Sure"—Zoey's voice was a mixture of sarcasm and outrage—"you took me back, all right. But you act totally cold!"

"Totally cold? Who spent the past two nights making you dinner?"

"You did—with *Kate*!"

"I wish you could hear yourself and how ridiculous you sound."

"Ridiculous? If I'm so ridiculous, why don't you come over to my house at night anymore? If I'm so ridiculous, why don't you want to have sex with me anymore?"

"What?" Lucas was almost screaming. "Make up your mind, Zoey! For months you treat me like I'm some sick pervert because I want to sleep with you. Then I decide to do things your way and stop giving you all that so-called pressure, and you're still not satisfied! What do you want from me, Zoey? I'd love to know!"

"For starters, you can stop going gaga over Kate!"

"I can't believe you, Zoey," Lucas said with a disgusted sigh.

Zoey felt a cold silence permeate the van.

Happy Valentine's Day, she thought.

After surveying the hotel room, Claire sat down on the end of the queen-sized bed. She reached for the bag she'd already unpacked and took out the one item remaining in it: her journal. She had just enough time to dash off a quick entry before heading over to the party and the night with Aaron that lay ahead.

February 14, 9:45 p.m.

I am sitting on the bed in room 928 of

the Portland Ritz-Carlton. I can hardly believe that within the next few hours I will be on this bed again, losing my virginity to Aaron. Whenever I think about it, a little shiver goes through my body. Who would believe that I, Claire Geiger, could feel so giddy? But that's the effect Aaron has on me. He makes me so excited, so happy. That's why I'm sure that he's the right person to be my first.

I've decided not to let him know this, though. Of course, he should figure out what I have in store for our night together pretty quickly, if he hasn't already guessed. But he doesn't know that it will be my first time. And I've decided not to tell him, at least not until it's already happened.

Why? A few reasons, actually. First of all, I don't want him to feel like he's too in control. I know he's had sex before, and I get the distinct feeling that Aaron would see the fact that I haven't as some kind of weakness or vulnerability on my part. Besides, I already know from reading the letter that girl sent him and from seeing him in action with Zoey that Aaron gets a kick out of conning the virginal type. I just want to make sure to keep the playing field level.

I'm not going to lie, though, and I fully intend to tell him after the deed is done. Besides, this way I can see if he can guess that it's my first time. It'll make the experience that much more memorable.

Claire glanced at the clock on the nightstand. She'd better leave if she wanted to make her entrance at the party when she'd planned to.

Claire shut her journal and put it and her bag in the back of the closet. As she closed its mirrored door, she cast one last glance at Claire Geiger the virgin and waved good-bye to her.

Twenty-two

"Excuse me," Zoey called as she made her way up the stairs.

Whoever was throwing this party sure knew a lot of people, but as of yet no one could tell Zoey where the bathroom was. Although she'd used it as an excuse to make a hasty departure from Lucas as soon as they'd arrived, Zoey was beginning to feel that she really had to go.

When she finally made her way up to the second-story landing, Zoey scanned the floor below her for Lucas. He was nowhere to be seen.

He must be off looking for his dear friend Kate.

"The bathroom's that way," shouted the girl on the steps whom Zoey had asked before.

"Thanks!" Zoey had to yell to be heard over the music. The Red Hot Chili Peppers were blasting from somewhere, which made her think of Nina. Zoey hoped her night with Benjamin was turning out better than Zoey's night with Lucas.

She made her way to the bathroom line and waited, thinking of the fight she and Lucas had been in for the last half of their drive down. Was this what their relationship was going to be from now on, a continuous cycle of cheating on each other? What was the point in even having a relationship if they didn't have a basic level of trust?

Zoey tapped her foot impatiently. The line was taking way too long. A house this big certainly had more than one toilet. There had to be another bathroom around there somewhere, and Zoey took off down the hall in search of it.

"Excuse me," she said, pushing her way through another group of bodies to turn into another hallway. To the right, a door was partially open.

It's probably a bedroom, but maybe it's got a bathroom inside, she reasoned as she made her way through the door.

Once inside, Zoey stepped back in shock. Not twenty feet away, Kate Levin stood kissing . . . Aaron Mendel?

Claire was acutely aware of the stares she received as she entered the party. If she hadn't already known she looked hot in her tight red velour shirt and black miniskirt, the appreciative looks from every guy in the room would have told her so.

Claire let a pleased smile form on her lips. Being the best-looking girl in the house had its advantages, but none that she was planning to capitalize on that night. She had bigger fish to fry.

She scanned the living room in search of Aaron but couldn't find him. As Claire turned to leave the room, she nearly caused Lucas to spill the extra glass of punch he had in his hand.

"Whoops!" she said as they both started laughing. "You should learn not to sneak up on people like that, Cabral." She had to shout over the music.

"And you should learn not to make such sudden movements at crowded parties," he yelled back.

"If you're looking for Zoey," she said, leaning in so that she didn't have to scream, "I didn't see her in there."

"I know," he replied. "She went upstairs to find the bathroom."

Claire nodded. Zoey was one of those girls who always headed for the bathroom. She was so predictable.

"You look great, Claire," Lucas said, giving her outfit an admiring glance. "Too bad you're wasting all that on a creep like Aaron Mendel."

Claire didn't expect Lucas to understand her feelings for Aaron. After all, thanks to Claire, Lucas had walked in on Aaron making out with Zoey. "Stop pouting, Lucas," she said in his ear. "You've already had your chance."

She pulled back to see Lucas's grinning face. He might be on the simple side, Claire thought, but she had to admit that Lucas could always appreciate a good line. She waved good-bye and took off to find Aaron.

There had been a time when she'd thought seriously about Lucas. He had been her first boyfriend, maybe even her first love. And he had spent two years in Youth Authority taking the rap for a crime she'd committed, which was kind of romantic when you thought about it. Claire even had the sense that she could take Lucas away from Zoey if she wanted. But she didn't want to. How could she, when she had Aaron? Unlike Lucas, he was her equal in every way. If only she could find him, Claire would show Aaron just how much he meant to her.

But where was he? Claire had timed her entrance to make sure that Aaron would have already arrived and been waiting for her—but not for too long. Surely he

166

had to be there somewhere, she figured as she tried to part the sea of bodies on the stairway.

"Have you seen Aaron Mendel?" Claire asked a guy in a plaid flannel shirt who had been eyeing her breasts.

"Who?" the guy asked, brushing against her as he leaned in to hear her better.

What a lame way to cop a feel, Claire thought as she fought back the temptation to slap him. Finding Aaron was her top priority, not putting this jerk in his place.

"Aaron Mendel. Have you seen him?" she repeated with all the patience she could muster.

"I think I saw him go up that way," the guy said, waving his beer toward a hallway to the right. "But that was a while ago."

"Thanks," Claire shouted as she made her way in the direction he had indicated. At least she was now certain that Aaron had arrived.

Claire turned the corner and, to her surprise, bumped right into a very stunned-looking Zoey.

"What's the matter?" Claire asked her, directing her gaze into the room Zoey had just come from.

But she didn't need to wait for an answer. Right in front of her, Aaron was making out with some redhead.

Making Out:
Aaron Lets Go

Book 14 in the explosive series about broken hearts, secrets, friendship, and of course, love.

First **Aaron** wanted **Zoey,** then he fell for **Claire,** but now he's ruined everything because of what happened with **Kate.** Somehow he must win **Claire** back—even if it means hurting **Kate.** But **Claire** may never love him again if…

Aaron
lets go

Calling all tEen ReaDers:

Do you like to read great books
featuring characters you can relate to?

Do you have strong opinions and lots of ideas
about books and reading?

Want to get free books, sneak previews,
and other stuff?